"Don't tempt me beyond my control, Tess,"

Carson warned.

She sensed he was near a turning point. "I'll try not to," she whispered. "But I have limits, too."

"I know."

He released her and stepped back. His eyes were suddenly bleak, the fires of a moment ago doused by thoughts she couldn't follow. She walked toward the tent, then glanced back and watched as he added more wood to the fire and checked the stallion to see if the animal was warm enough.

They were alike, she thought, the man and the beast. Both of them wild creatures who couldn't be forced, not without breaking their spirit. She'd never do that. Each of them must give his trust to her of his own accord.

She'd wait.

Wrangler Dads
1. *Madeleine's Cowboy*
Kristine Rolofson
2. *Cowboy's Kin*
Victoria Pade
3. *Trouble at Lone Spur*
Roz Denny Fox
4. *Upon a Midnight Clear*
Lynn Erickson
5. *Cowboy at the Wedding*
Karen Rose Smith
6. *Dangerous*
Caroline Cross
Reunion Western-Style!
7. *Rodeo Rider*
Stella Bagwell
8. *Mustang Valley*
Jackie Merritt
9. *Holding on to Alex*
Margaret Way
10. *Home Fires Burning Bright*
Laurie Paige
11. *One More Rodeo*
Lynnette Kent
12. *The Reckoning*
Joleen Daniels
Conveniently Wed
13. *Seduction of the Reluctant Bride*
Barbara McCauley
14. *Temporary Husband*
Day Leclaire
15. *The Wilde Bunch*
Barbara Boswell
16. *Her Torrid Temporary Marriage*
Sara Orwig
17. *The Newlywed Game*
Bonnie K. Winn
18. *Gideon's Bride*
Amelia Autin
Holding Out for a Hero
19. *Midnight Prey*
Caroline Burnes
20. *Bulletproof Heart*
Sheryl Lynn
21. *Hiding Out at the Circle C*
Jill Shalvis
22. *Lucky Devil*
Patricia Rosemoor
23. *She Caught the Sheriff*
Anne Marie Duquette
24. *The Unlikely Bodyguard*
Amy J. Fetzer
Rawhide & Lace
25. *Cowboys Are for Loving*
Marie Ferrarella
26. *The Rancher and the Redhead*
Allison Leigh
27. *White Gold*
Curtiss Ann Matlock
28. *Texas Dawn*
Joan Elliott Pickart
29. *Rancher's Choice*
Kylie Brant
30. *Delightful Jones*
Patricia Knoll
Kids & Kin
31. *The Troublemaker Bride*
Leanne Banks
32. *Cowboys Do It Best*
Eileen Wilks
33. *The Rancher and the Baby*
Elizabeth August
34. *Boss Lady and the Hired Hand*
Barbara McMahon
35. *The Cowboy's Courtship*
Patricia Thayer
36. *The Farmer Takes a Wife*
Jodi O'Donnell
Men of the Land
37. *The Badlands Bride*
Rebecca Winters
38. *The Cowboy Wants a Wife!*
Susan Fox
39. *Woman at Willagong Creek*
Jessica Hart
40. *Wyoming Wife?*
Shawna Delacorte
41. *Cowboys, Babies and Shotgun Vows*
Shirley Rogers
42. *Home Is Where Hank Is*
Martha Shields
Secrets!
43. *The Rancher's Runaway Bride*
Judith Bowen
44. *Midnight Cowboy*
Adrianne Lee
45. *Remember Me, Cowboy*
Caroline Burnes
46. *The Other Laura*
Sheryl Lynn
47. *A Man without Love*
Beverly Bird
48. *The Return of the Cowboy*
Cheryl Biggs

HOME FIRES BURNING BRIGHT

Laurie Paige

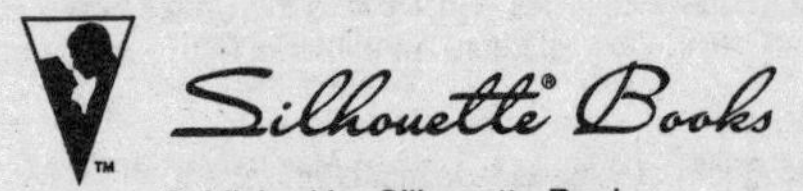

Published by Silhouette Books
America's Publisher of Contemporary Romance

ISBN: 0-373-65319-0

HOME FIRES BURNING BRIGHT

First Silhouette Books printing July 1990

Visit Silhouette Books at www.eHarlequin.com

Printed in U.S.A.

LAURIE PAIGE

"One of the nicest things about writing romances is researching locales, careers and ideas. In the interest of authenticity, most writers will try anything...once." Along with her writing adventures, Laurie has been a NASA engineer, a past president of the Romance Writers of America, a mother and a grandmother. She was twice a Romance Writers of America RITA® Award finalist for Best Traditional Romance and has won awards from *Romantic Times* for Best Silhouette Special Edition and Best Silhouette in addition to appearing on the *USA TODAY* bestseller list. Recently resettled in Northern California, Laurie is looking forward to whatever experiences her next novel will send her on.

For my friend Tessa,
fellow adventurer
and marshmallow-roaster extraordinaire.

Chapter One

Tess Garrick's breath fogged into a small cloud in front of her face when she stepped out of the Clark-dale post office. Snow from the last storm lay in ragged drifts along the street, and the clouds promised another blizzard before the day was over. Spring was only a week away.

Tell that to the weatherman, she mocked silently as she walked down the street perusing the stack of mail, which was mostly advertisements.

A garish postcard from her half sister, Lainie, was tucked in among the flyers. She scanned it eagerly. Lainie and her family were in warm, sunny Hawaii. "Wish you were here," Lainie had written. Me, too, Tess thought. Anyplace south had to be better than north-central Arizona at this time of the year.

She took a step and her foot hit…air.

Tess sprawled forward with the fleeting hope that

no cars were coming up the slippery side street while she pitched headlong onto the pavement. Just as suddenly as she lurched forward, she was propelled backward to safety.

A strong arm clamped across her middle like an iron bar, and she was pinned securely against the tall, rangy frame of a man. Instinctively she knew who it was and let her head rest against his shoulder for a second, her heart pounding with relief at being saved and with excitement at being held by him.

"Carson," she said, warmth suffusing her from some deep inner core. "Thank you for saving me. That could have been a nasty fall." She smiled up at him, their mouths very close.

At five feet eight inches, she was only five inches shorter than he was. It would have been a simple thing for him to tilt his head forward a bit more and for her to stretch up on tiptoe...

"Why the hell don't you watch where you're going?" Carson McCumber snarled at her, thrusting her aside as soon as he'd moved them away from the three steps down to the street.

She remembered other times when he'd put her away from him. And another when he hadn't.

Once, he'd held her as if he'd never let her go and poured kisses all over her face. Once, his mouth had touched hers with such rapacious hunger it had almost frightened her...a man's hunger...a man's passion.

She'd been seventeen: he'd been twenty-three, a hard-working ranch hand on the Garrick family spread. Because of her, he'd gotten fired from the job. That had been five years ago.

Since that time, she'd finished high school and college and come back home to live, but whenever she and Carson met, he looked at her with eyes like granite.

Which was the way he was looking at her now. She fixed a bright smile on her face, determined that he wouldn't know he still had the power to hurt her.

"I was reading a post card from my sister. See?" Tess held the card up to him, so he could view all the gorgeous hunks on their surfboards, riding the white-foaming waves.

"If you can't wait until you get home to read your mail, you'd better read it at the post office," he advised, and walked off.

She watched him go. He dressed as most ranchers did in these parts—boots, jeans, flannel shirt and sheepskin jacket. Over his dark, unruly hair, he wore the usual Stetson, its brim shielding his dark eyes.

He was as strong as she remembered, but thinner. The finely molded bones of his angular face seemed to protrude against the bronzed skin. He needed some home cooking and some looking after, she thought with a tenderness she couldn't suppress.

"Have a nice day," she called to his back.

He hesitated a fraction, then went on.

"You, too," she said to herself as she descended the three steps and crossed the street to the ranch wagon, which was loaded with groceries.

She felt a slight pain in her stomach and dug an antacid tablet out of her purse. She chewed it and swallowed. For a minute she laid an arm over the steering wheel and rested her forehead against it.

The doctor at the college clinic had warned her about burning her candle at both ends. She had tried to load up as many courses as possible so she could earn her credits and get back home. Which was where she had really wanted to be.

Everyone in her family had insisted that she finish her education and learn something of the world other than this one spot in Arizona. Carson had bluntly told her to get out of his life.

"You're too young to know what you want," he had said. "You find me interesting because I'm somewhat different...and forbidden. How many men have you known? You've grown up with the boys around here since kindergarten."

He had doubted her love. That had hurt, but his rejection had been the deciding factor in her life. She had gritted her teeth and finished school, including college, with high marks. She had dated regularly—the captain of the basketball team, the captain of the debate team, premed students, prelaw students, a graduate engineer. When she had earned enough credits to graduate, she left it all without a backward glance.

Funny, now she was home—all educated, she supposed—and had all the time in the world, but her stomach still ached.

She sighed and tried to school her face to poker blankness, knowing her emotions were usually all too visible, before she drove over to the bank to finish the ranch business. All she needed was for one of the town gossips to see her looking upset and start speculating on the cause.

Lord, but she was ready for spring. In the two months since she'd returned to the Garrick Valley Ranch north of the town, she had experienced two natural blizzards and several man-made ones—the latter being the cold rebuffs she had received from Carson every time they met.

Carson. He'd changed since she went off to the university. Gone was the cowboy who had looked at her with such yearning in his eyes...who'd put her away from him and told her he didn't want her to come around, ever again.

The raw hurt of that parting lingered in her heart, a thorn that pricked at unexpected moments, like when he had saved her a few minutes ago.

Now he was all stern, rugged male, steely-eyed and ruthless, with no time for the tenderness of loving...or even the brief mindlessness of passion. She knew. She'd flirted with him when he showed up at the dance last week, had even followed him outside and tried a little seduction. Apparently nothing could daunt his icy self-possession nowadays. Certainly not her.

Not you, not you, her heart echoed.

No, not me, she acknowledged. Carson, the young man she'd loved, the one who'd loved her back for a short time, had gone. She didn't know the man who now claimed the name.

A knock on the window brought her head up.

Carson leaned down. "Are you all right?" His breath frosted the window on the outside for a second before the cold, dry air evaporated the moisture.

She cranked the window open. "That's privileged

information,'' she said, keeping her voice light and getting the smile back on her face. ''It'll cost you to find out.''

A tiny movement in his jaw caught her attention. He was probably grinding his teeth and wishing he could grind her up and spit her out of his life. Well, that was one of the problems of living in a ranching community. You kept running into everybody.

''I'm fine,'' she said.

''You'd better get home. The weather report calls for snow later this afternoon.''

''Worried that you might have to rescue me?'' She grimaced at the idea. He'd probably perform some superhuman task to get her back to her place and then get himself home so he wouldn't have to bother with her. ''I'll be okay. I've driven in snow.''

A mysterious emotion appeared briefly in his eyes, a darker shadow among other dark shadows. What was he thinking?

To her amazement, a smile appeared on his face, a rather grim one, but most assuredly a smile. He looked incredibly handsome as twin slashes appeared at either side of his mouth. ''Quite the competent rancher, huh?''

''Of course.'' She tilted her chin up, not sure how to take this new mood. Her smile felt stiff on her lips. He was looking at her mouth, she realized and clamped down on a desire to lick her lips. She wouldn't be provocative again. He'd left the dance in a fury after ordering her to stay inside ''where it was safe.''

Wasn't she safe around him? The way he acted, a

whole harem of naked women would be safe with him.

He heaved a deep sigh as if giving up on some internal argument with himself. "You want a cup of coffee and piece of pie over at Nell's?"

Tess stared at him.

He impatiently pushed the brim of his hat off his forehead. "You might need some reserve energy going home if it gets as cold as the news says it's going to."

"Yes, I—" she had to clear her throat "—I'll meet you there. I have some banking to do. It won't take long."

He nodded, looking as if he already regretted the offer. Well, too bad, Mr. McCumber. You asked and now you're stuck with me. She grinned at him and rolled the window up.

When he stepped aside, she started the engine and headed for the drive-in window at the bank. The chore was finished in record time. She parked and walked to the popular café. Homemade apple pie with cinnamon, she thought. And cheese melting over it. She had read that a liking for desserts indicated a sensuous nature. She was definitely in the mood for dessert.

He was waiting at the café when she arrived.

They went in, hung their coats and hats on a peg and took a seat at a table for two next to the window. The distant mountains were solid white, every pine branch weighted with snow.

"Looks like this year is making up for the drought of the last three," she said, glancing at him with a smile.

"Yes," he said.

He picked up the menu and studied it until the waitress came over. So much for brilliant conversation, Tess quipped to herself, refusing to be daunted by the return of his dark mood.

"Apple pie, heated, with cheese, please," she ordered.

He glanced at her, then ordered ham and eggs and coffee.

"I'd like coffee, too. Decaffeinated," Tess added, remembering her stomach.

After the waitress poured them each a cup of coffee and left with their orders, Carson leaned back in his seat and studied Tess. "You preferred milk once upon a time, as I recall."

She remembered, too. It had been at this café during Easter vacation. He had teased her when she ordered a glass of milk, which was also one of his favorite beverages. "Growing girls still need their calcium," he had remarked.

"Look again," she had tossed right back. "I'm all grown up."

What a lot she'd still had to learn at seventeen. Such as, love didn't conquer all; sometimes not anything, it seemed.

Tess felt the familiar burning in her middle and pressed a hand there as if to hold the pain back. Studying too hard wasn't the only thing that could cause incipient ulcers. Thinking of Carson and the past could, too. She'd been wrong, she decided. He'd wanted her, but he hadn't loved her.

When the waitress filled their water glasses, Tess

took a big swallow and felt it slide coolly down her throat, putting out the flames of memory and lost love.

She sighed, then glanced up to encounter Carson's hard gaze. His eyes, like his hair, were very dark, almost black, yet with unexpected highlights in both. She had seen his eyes glow with inner emotion, or perhaps it had only been passion.

"What is it?" he asked, frowning. "What's wrong with you?"

"Nothing. Why? Am I turning green or something?"

He shook his head, a quick gesture of impatience. "You act as if you're in pain." There was a question at the end of the statement.

"Oh, that," she said airily. "Ulcers. The hazard of modern times."

"You have ulcers?" He looked incredulous.

"Not yet." She laughed, tossing off the remark. "I'm just...tense. For some people that turns into heart attacks, for others, ulcers. Rarely do people get both. If that's true, then I should be safe from heart disease. I get a tummy ache when I get tense."

His eyes had narrowed as she gave her little spiel, now they seemed to smolder as he looked her over. "Are you tense now?"

"I must be," she said flippantly, and took another sip of water. At least her hands didn't shake.

"Dammit," he barked, startling her, "don't play games. I'm in no mood for them. Are you in pain?"

Tess wiped a drop of sloshed water off her chin. "I'm fine, Carson. Really."

He nodded, not quite believing her. "Do I...does it upset you to be around me?" he asked, his voice going soft and deep.

Don't be nice, don't be gentle, don't pity me, she wanted to tell him, but she only shook her head. "Of course not. You're a neighbor and an old friend. Why should I be upset?"

He looked as if he'd like to pursue the subject, but their food arrived just then. The waitress served them, poured more coffee and left. Carson picked up his fork and began on his meal.

"Didn't you eat breakfast this morning?" she asked, noting the way he was devouring the eggs and ham.

"Yeah, at about four."

"Early hours," she commented, taking a bite of pie. It was delicious, warm and melting on her tongue.

"A cow was having trouble."

"Umm." She understood about cows and horses and birthing. Living her entire life on a ranch had given her more than a nodding acquaintance with the facts of life. She loved the whole process of seasons and cycles—dormant winter, reviving spring, lush summer, bountiful fall. Mating, birthing, dying—the never-ending cycle of life.

"I love it, don't you?" she asked, her eyes taking on a misty glow. "Each season unfolding, bringing forth its goodness—"

Carson snorted. "Is that the way you see it? I'd think you'd know better. Only city dudes who'd never tried to keep a herd alive in a blizzard talk like that. Out before dawn in weather that would freeze your buns off, slogging through mud up to your knees with a howling wind blowing right through you...yeah, that's real fun."

Tess saw a momentary bleakness in his eyes before he smiled. Such a cynical smile. When had he lost his dreams?

"A poet once wrote, 'Here he lies where he longed to be: Home is the sailor, home from the sea; And the hunter, home from the hill.'" She blinked the mist from her eyes. "Only I'd change it to, here she *lives* where she longed to be."

Carson looked out the window at the hills, his thoughts hidden behind a hard composure. He seemed so distant.

"So, yes," she concluded, "I'm glad to be home, no matter how many blizzards I have to endure."

"You're young yet," he said. "I was homesick when I went away to the university, too."

It angered her that he persisted in seeing her as a student, a youngster still wet behind the ears. She'd paid her dues. "I'm out of college now, in case you didn't know," she informed him.

She tried to imagine him homesick but failed. He was too self-sufficient to ever miss anyone. Of course, there was his ranch. He loved it, or he had, once.

One time, when they'd shared dreams, he'd told her he wanted to build it into the thriving enterprise it had been in his grandfather's day, before his father had ruined the place with his drinking and spendthrift ways. Carson had been working on her family's ranch, trying to earn enough money to make repairs and start a new herd on his land.

He had talked to her, telling her of his plans and his hopes for the future. He'd also kissed her. Her half brother had happened upon them and sent Carson packing.

She closed her eyes, unable to bear the pain and beauty of that memory. Once, when she'd gone into town for the Saturday-night dance, she'd followed him to the motel where he was spending the night, not an unusual thing among the cowboys who sometimes drank too much when they came to town. Her brother had followed her there, too. The humiliation of being sent to the car while the men talked had been terrible. Carson had avoided her after that.

"Was it because of Dev?" she asked, opening her eyes to find Carson looking intently at her. He glanced away. "Was he why you wouldn't see me anymore?"

He had no difficulty understanding her thoughts. "You were too young. Jailbait. I wasn't having any part of that."

"I'm an adult now," she reminded him.

"Then you should know better than to hang around broke cowboys." He glanced outside, muttered an imprecation and stood, taking a couple of bills out of a very worn leather wallet and dropping them on the table. "Come on. We have to go."

"Shall I offer to pay for my part?"

"I can still manage the price of a piece of pie and a cup of coffee." He grinned without humor. "For another month or two, at any rate. After that, it might be a strain."

"What happens in a month or two?" she asked,

curious about his life and determined to inquire while he was willing to answer.

"A large payment on a larger debt. Don't pretend you don't know," he said in a hard voice.

"I don't." Why should she know?

He didn't say more. He held her coat for her while she put it on and handed her the woolly toboggan hat she liked to wear. Her mother had knitted it the winter before she died and had given it to Tess for Christmas. It was red and white with a big red pompon.

Out on the street, they both buttoned up tight against the wind. Snow was just starting to fall, big feathery flakes that sifted down out of the heavens.

"Thanks for the treat," Tess said, stopping by her vehicle.

Carson started to say something but changed his mind. "You're welcome," he said instead. He surveyed the sky once more. The clouds were thick, the snow steady. "I have to stop by the feed store. Wait for me. I'll follow you home."

"That's okay. It's too far out of your way."

"I'll take the dirt road over the ridge to my house."

"Really, Carson, I'll be all right—"

"For once, just do something without arguing," he snapped, jamming his hands into his pockets.

Tess fought her own anger. Deliberately choosing the lighter side of life, she folded her hands beneath her chin as if praying, and lowered her eyelashes. "Yes, my lord and master," she intoned. "I live to obey."

When she looked up, it was to catch a suspicious

twitch at the corners of his mouth. She kept her own mouth straight.

"See that you do. Meet me at the store."

Fifteen minutes later she was on the road to the ranch, a fifty-minute drive in good weather, a sometimes impossible one in bad. Right now it was so-so. The new snow wasn't thick enough to be a serious threat, neither did it help driving conditions.

Nor did having an autocratic male boring holes into the back of your head, Tess grumbled to herself as she turned the wagon onto the ranch road, Carson right behind her in his pickup.

"Will you be able to get over the ridge?" she asked when he pulled up beside her at her house. Worry ate at her insides.

"Yeah, I'll put her in four-wheel drive."

"Men," she complained aloud. "You think you're invincible. Come in for lunch, then head back on the main road this afternoon. The plows will keep it clear until dark."

Carson shook his head. "Thanks, but I have work to do. Don't go out anymore today. This is more than just a flurry." He rolled up the window and drove off.

"Thanks for the helpful advice," she muttered. "With Carson McCumber around, who needs Abby or Ann?"

A lone figure was walking around the paddocks when Tess pulled under the carport next to the mud room and kitchen. She waved when Rose looked toward her. The other woman came over.

Rose was twenty-one, a widow who had arrived at

the ranch two days ago to visit her father. And recover from her grief, Tess assumed. They had known each other long ago, when they were girls.

"Hi. Need a hand?" Rose asked.

"Sure do. That crate has eggs," Tess said. "Help me carry it into the house. It's too heavy for one."

It was amazing, the number of eggs a bunch of cowhands could consume in a month. Tess had tried to warn them about cholesterol to no avail. Zed, Rose's father and the ranch foreman, had just looked at her and continued his breakfast—three eggs, two sausage links and four pieces of bacon, as usual. He'd been eating the same thing for almost sixty years. He wasn't apt to change to bran flakes with banana slices at her exhortation.

Cowboys. Don't ever fall in love with one.

The two women carried the month's supply of groceries into the huge pantry off the mud room, laughing over the amount of edibles.

In a pinch, Tess figured she could feed the crew for three or four months without great difficulty. She had taken over the household responsibilities since Agnes, their housekeeper, had gone to Texas to stay with her daughter during a difficult pregnancy.

When Tess and Rose finished, Tess stood back and admired the orderly rows of canned and dried food, the two freezers, one bulging with meat, the other with vegetables and fruit, and the jars of homemade jellies and jams preserved by Agnes.

"I love it when we have enough food to stand a siege," Tess remarked to Rose. "As if the ranch could face the world and not back down."

Rose nodded. "To have your own land around you and owe nobody, that is many men's dream."

"Come have some coffee. How about a sandwich? It's nearly time for lunch. We could have a gabfest. I've hardly seen you since you arrived."

Tess glanced at her childhood chum, who was six months younger than herself, yet had already experienced a great tragedy in her life. Her husband had dashed out to the quick market three months ago to buy a pack of cigarettes. The place was robbed while he was there. He and the clerk had been shot and killed. The robber was never found.

"Was that what you and your husband wanted?" Tess asked gently.

"No, we were happy in our little apartment. He liked working for the telephone company. He was the first of his family to have a skilled job...not to work in the fields."

"I see."

Tess knew that Jose's parents had migrated from one of the South American countries. Rose, whose mother had left Zed years ago because she couldn't stand the loneliness of ranch life, had also worked at the phone company.

"How long are you going to stay with your father?"

"I'm thinking of living here," Rose said.

"Oh? I'm surprised. You were only eight when your mother left. You grew up in L.A."

"This was always home, too, just as my mother's house was. I want to get away from the city. So much violence."

"Yes. Sit down while I put the mail in the office. Hey, how about putting on a pot of coffee?" Tess knew that would make her friend feel at home. As Tess skimmed down the hall to the office and back, she wondered if Rose had come home to hide from life.

Had *she*? she questioned herself. What was she going to do with her business degree? Take over the operation of Lainie's gift shop in town? The ranch didn't need her when Dev was there to run things.

"Oh, here's a card from my sister, Lainie. Look at all these gorgeous men. Maybe we should take us a vacation in Hawaii, Rose, and see what we can catch."

Tess handed over the post card.

Rose looked at the front and read the back. She laughed. "These are not men. They are handsome boys. I think they should be thrown back into the sea and allowed to grow some more."

"Hmm, you think their minds haven't caught up with their bodies?" Tess studied the post card again.

In her inner vision, she saw another man, one dark and exciting, determined, even harsh in his approach to life. Carson would make a perfect highwayman. She could see him in black, with a bandanna hiding his mouth, which was rather thin but wide, and definitely sensuous. His dark eyes would be full of mocking laughter as he robbed the stagecoach.

If she were a passenger, would he abduct her, unable to let her go after gazing into her eyes? Get real, she admonished her imagination. Carson would toss her aside without a second thought.

"Yes," Rose agreed.

Tess opened a can of tuna fish. "Tuna salad okay for lunch, or do you want something heavier?"

"Tuna sounds fine."

"Good. I met Carson McCumber in town. He and I had pie and coffee before coming home, so I'm not very hungry."

"McCumber. I don't remember him," Rose mused.

"He worked for us one summer. That was five years ago. His place is the next one over the ridge."

"Umm, I see."

Tess suspected her friend saw too much. "Here, our sandwiches are ready. Do you want soda, milk or coffee with yours?"

"Soda will be fine."

While they ate, they caught up on each other's lives since they had last talked. It brought back memories of happier times for both of them.

"And you, Tess. Where is your husband?" Rose finally asked.

"There's no one for me."

Rose studied her friend. "No one?" she asked softly.

Tess grimaced. "No one who counts. I'll tell you someday. Right now, I've got to get to work. There are bills to be paid and ledgers to update."

They walked to the door. "If you hear of any jobs, I might be interested," Rose said. "Keep me in mind."

"Right."

After Rose left, Tess went into the ranch office to

arrange the bills in order of payment and to make out the checks.

The fact that she could take over the books was one reason Dev had insisted on taking Lainie and Davie, their four-year-old son, to Hawaii. Lainie had lost a child in the winter, then caught a bad case of the flu. Dev had taken her to the sunshine to recover.

Tess thought of the deep love that had developed between Dev and Lainie after Dev's father married Lainie's mother. Dev and Lainie, too, had survived a long, difficult period before they could admit their feelings. In fact, it was their concern for Tess—their willful half-sister—that had brought them together five years ago.

Sudden tears filled her eyes. Would she ever find a love like that? She brushed the moisture out of her eyes roughly. There was no use in feeling sorry for herself. Carson had made it perfectly clear that she wasn't welcome in his life. Sometimes, when he was so cold and distant with her, she felt she hated him.

But then she remembered how hard his life had been compared to hers, and her anger would melt. Once, she had seen him driving his father home from town although he had been too young to have a license at that time. He must have been about fourteen. His face had been so tense, his dignity so fragile.

Sighing, she got out the check book and the ranch ledgers. Time to get down to the practical side of things.

She wrote the checks and made the bookkeeping entries. When she finished, she picked up the last unopened letter and studied it, uncertain what to do. It was addressed to Lainie.

The left-hand corner contained a rural-route and box number, but no name. A local rancher, she assumed. It was probably business. But what if it were personal? What personal dealings could Lainie have with a nearby rancher? It had to be ranch stuff.

She stared at the envelope. If the person had only put a name on the darned thing, then she'd have known what to do. She considered the return address. The route was the same as the Garrick ranch. The box number rang no bells, but she never remembered those.

The Moreleys to the west of them? The McCumber place was due east. Carson wouldn't write Lainie. She tore open the letter.

It was business. From Carson.

Tess gasped aloud as she read. He wouldn't be able to make any payment on the loan this year, but would pay the interest in the fall after he sold his beeves. If that wasn't satisfactory, Lainie was to let him know and he would try to make other arrangements to repay the loan.

Tess read the letter once, twice and a third time. Her hands were shaking when she finished. Carson owed Lainie money, a lot of money. She gazed into space and tried to absorb the news. A gleam appeared in her eyes.

She had an idea.

No, she couldn't do it. He'd never forgive her. He'd really hate her. He'd shoot her for sure.

But if she... She pressed a hand to her stomach,

not because it was hurting, but because it was full of butterflies. Oh, if she only dared to do what she was thinking!

Did she have the courage?

Was she a Garrick or not!

Tess went to the safe and twirled the combination. A few minutes later, she was sitting on the floor in front of the open safe, papers spread out neatly around her.

She found the document she was searching for and read it. Taking it to the telephone, she dialed Zed's number. Rose answered.

"Rose, this is Tess. Can you come up here a minute? I think I have a job for you."

Rose arrived breathless, her curiosity aroused. She took one look at the brilliant gleam in Tess's eyes.

"I think you're up to something" Rose said. "I seem to remember that look...just before you got us into trouble...with your father, with the teacher, with the pastor at church—"

Tess threw back her head and laughed. "I've just found the secret to happiness." Her smile became stubborn.

"Tell me. I could use it."

"Only my happiness. I think." Tess closed the safe and turned to her old comrade-in-hot-water. "Rose, could you take care of the horses, plan the menus, cook and keep the bunkhouse kitchen supplied until Dev and Lainie get back?"

Rose looked bemused. "What are *you* going to be doing?"

"Working at the next ranch over the ridge. I'll tell

you about it later, if everything works out. Could you take over here for me?''

The young widow shrugged and grinned. ''Sure.''

''It's pretty cold in the mornings, feeding and watering the stable stock. Maybe Zed can hire some part-time help.''

''No need. I'll do it. Now tell me your plan.''

Tess told her what she wanted to do. Rose rolled her eyes heavenward and asked that God be sure and watch out for children and fools. Her friend needed all the help she could get.

''What time is it in Hawaii? Earlier or later than we are?'' Tess demanded, jumping up from the sofa and heading for the telephone on the office desk.

''Four or five hours earlier, maybe. I don't know for sure.''

''It doesn't matter. I'm going to call anyway.'' She picked up the telephone and dialed the number of the resort where her sister was staying.

Rose waved and tiptoed out, heading back to her father's house. Tess called goodbye just as the phone was picked up on the other end. A woman answered.

''Lainie? Oh, good, just the person I wanted to talk to. I have an offer you can't refuse.''

At five that afternoon, Tess put down the receiver for the last time. The instrument was hot and her ear felt as if it were about to fall off. She rubbed it intently.

If everything went okay—it was just a matter of signing some legal documents—she would soon own about one-fifth interest in the McCumber ranch. She'd just bought the note from her sister.

Looking at Carson's erratic payments, Tess realized the last five years hadn't been kind to him. The ranch obviously hadn't done as well in reality as it had in his dreams.

For a second, pity overwhelmed her. He'd had such grand visions of how he'd fixed up the ranch and make it as profitable as it had been years ago. Yeah, she knew about dreams.

She got up and went to the window. The intense cold reached in through the glass and penetrated her flesh, causing chill bumps.

Or were they induced by fright because of what she'd done that afternoon? Carson was apt to strangle her when she told him.

One thing for sure, he couldn't run her off now.

Chapter Two

Spring began on a snowy Monday. Carson reined in the brown gelding under a tree and pulled off a thick glove. He blew on his fingers to warm them, pulled a tiny notebook from his pocket and added the tally.

The calves killed by the blizzard numbered more than had survived. Any hopes he'd had of a profit this year went up in smoke like a blade of buffalo grass in a wildfire.

He tucked the pencil into the notebook spiral and stuck it back in his pocket. After pulling on his glove, he sat there for a minute, out of the wind, his mind a blank while he gazed at the ridge to the west of his spread.

Beyond it lay one of the most successful ranches in the state. Garrick Valley Ranch. He doubted if any of their calves had died. Dev Garrick had the money and the men to take care of his stock.

Well, there was no use in thinking about the Garricks and their ranch. He had his own to contend with.

He came upon another carcass on the way to the house and added it to the total. Damn. Damn. Damn.

At the ranch house, he fed the gelding and turned it loose in a paddock. Half a day was all a horse could take in this weather. He smiled grimly. Only man kept on and on, working past exhaustion into a mindless stupor. Sometimes he had come to, only to wonder what he was doing at a particular place at that particular time.

He went into the house. A pot of soup bubbled on the back burner. That had been one of his better ideas—to keep soup going all the time so he could grab a bite whenever he came to the house. He sat down at the old oak table with a huge bowl of it, a box of crackers and a glass of milk.

The milk reminded him of last week. Tess.

She had changed, whether for better or worse, he couldn't say, but she was different from five years ago. She was a woman now, no doubt of that. Even thick winter clothes couldn't disguise the smooth curves of her body.

At the thought of her, his own body reacted, surging strongly into readiness, letting him know he wasn't a monk. Although that sure as hell was the way he lived. He looked around the kitchen.

The sink was chipped and stained, full of dirty dishes. He'd do those tonight. The cabinets needed sanding and repainting or staining. The linoleum should have been replaced years ago. It was worn all the way through to the subflooring in some places.

He'd thought he would have the house all fixed up by now.

Well, it had a new roof. At least he no longer woke up with snow on his quilt. But that was all he had been able to do.

Five years.

A big chunk out of a man's life, especially when he worked sixteen to eighteen hour days and had no more to show for it than a new roof.

He stared across the room, seeing nothing but more years of the same drudgery ahead. Once, he'd let himself dream of bringing a wife home. Now...

Dreams are for starry-eyed kids, he reminded himself sharply. He had only cold, hard facts, and he'd better keep them in mind.

Tess's face appeared before his eyes. For a second, he saw her there, sitting across the table from him, looking at him out of her seventeen-year-old eyes. Ah, the way she used to look at him. All that adoration. All that fire and devotion.

She was so pretty with her brown hair the color of toast, with both dark and golden tones in it. Even her eyes were a sort of golden brown. Toast with honey, he thought, a smile playing across his mouth.

When she smiled, a tiny dimple appeared high on her left cheek. A honey of a girl. Honey-girl. Tess.

His eyes burned, and the vision left him.

What was wrong with her now? Tension, she had said. She had never been one to hold her feelings in. That had been part of the problem, one of the reasons she'd been so hard to resist. She looked at a man with all the love in the world in her eyes. He'd wanted to take it, to soak it up into his pores until he was saturated, until his soul was filled. God, yes, he'd wanted her....

He shoved back from the table, leaving his soup cooling in the bowl, his milk untouched. A person could drive himself crazy thinking of what might have been. He had to keep in mind what *was*. Which was nothing, not between Carson McCumber and Tess Garrick. The rich, pampered, headstrong Tess Garrick.

No one knew that better than he did. So you don't have to remind me, he snarled at his conscience. He wasn't about to get involved with her. No, sir. No way.

He put on his heavy sheepskin coat and wool hat. There were all those carcasses to be hauled in. The ones that were still frozen could be sold for pet food or glue; the others he'd have to skin out and sell for leather. If he worked until his mind was numb, he wouldn't think of Tess, one ridge over.

Tess chewed on her lower lip. She stopped and reminded herself not to do that. Her lip was developing a raw spot. Everything was in order. The ranch was in capable hands. She'd only have to come over once a month to pay the bills.

"Well, Rose, wish me luck," she said, giving her friend a fatalistic smile.

"You'll need it. I tried to get Dad to hand over his lucky rabbit's foot, but he wouldn't part with it."

"Thanks anyway. Well, I'm off." Tess stood there.

The two women gazed at each other. They started

laughing and threw their arms around each other for a final hug.

"Don't take no for an answer," Rose advised, her eyes teary.

"I won't. I'm a partner and I have a right to be there."

When Tess arrived at the McCumber place an hour later, she reminded herself of that fact several times.

Tess parked her red Mustang in the gravel verge at the back of the house. The place looked deserted. In fact, it looked abandoned. It hadn't had a coat of paint in years. In several places, the wood was completely bare and exposed to the elements. It had turned a silvery gray.

Other than five or six horses in the paddock, there didn't seem to be any other living thing around—no scampering dog running out to bark a welcome or growl a warning, no chickens huddled against the arctic blasts of wind that blew over the snow. Well, chickens would be in a chicken house. It was too cold for any creature to be outside today.

The blizzard had finally let up three days ago. The sun had come out strong and blinding on the fresh fall of snow, but the wind just whipped right through a person.

Gripping the door handle, Tess forced herself out of the warm car into the cold. Carrying a suitcase in each hand, she headed for the nearest door.

It opened into a kitchen-dining room that ran the width of the house. Windows all along the back wall faced southeast to take advantage of the morning sun for warmth and light. It was now early afternoon and only a bit of sun shone through the uncurtained windows.

She set her cases down and listened. Not a sound. The hair rose on the back of her neck. A soup bowl and glass of milk were on the table, as if some unknown person had prepared it for her, knowing she was coming. She felt like the heroine in a low-budget horror film.

Taking a very deep breath, she picked up her luggage and went in search of the bedroom. She'd been here once before. Smiling grimly, she remembered her brother stomping in, hot on her trail again. Dev wouldn't show up this time. Come what may between her and Carson, she couldn't expect a rescue at the eleventh hour. She was on her own.

She decided this was a B Western instead of a horror movie. Or maybe both. Carson would probably murder her.

The master bedroom was where she remembered. Looking at the bed's tousled covers, she knew Carson was using it. She chose another. It had a feminine tone with faded wall paper of large cabbage roses and a cherry bedstead and furniture. She swiped a finger over the dresser. It hadn't been dusted in a while.

She opened one case and stored its contents in the dresser drawers, then she hung the rest of her stuff in the closet. She'd brought mostly woolens, jeans and warm clothes. This was a working ranch, not a resort, and she intended to take part.

She returned to the kitchen and sat down at the table. Since lunch was ready, she might as well eat.

The soup was cool, the milk tepid, but she consumed them rapidly. She was hungry, and there was obviously lots of work to be done. She'd start with the stack of dishes in the sink as soon as she finished the meal.

Four hours later, the kitchen was spic and span, even the cabinet shelves wiped out and the dishes restacked in neat order.

A new pot simmered on the back burner. Chicken and dumplings. She'd found a plastic-wrapped package of chicken in the old chest-type freezer in the pantry. The chicken had had a bad case of freezer burn, so she'd thawed it, removed the skin and leathery parts, chopped it and stewed it to tenderness. She'd added the dumplings to the pot just a few minutes ago.

She glanced at the clock over the stove. At least the stove was a fairly modern gas range, and the refrigerator, while an older model, worked just fine. Washed inside and out, it gleamed in the soft light from old-fashioned wagon-wheel light fixtures, which had also been washed and shined.

It was past five. What time did Carson come in to eat?

A whicker from the stable reminded Tess of the animals. She pulled on her old sheepskin jacket and went out to tend them.

The stable was in good repair, she found. New boards had recently replaced old ones. The stalls were clean. She let the horses in, then fed and watered the five animals. After mucking out the fresh manure and spreading a bed of straw, she checked the other buildings. A barn with equipment stored in it. A shed with harness and garden tools. A blacksmith lean-to. If there had ever been a bunkhouse, it was gone.

Walking back to the house, she thought over the implications. There hadn't been any sign of another person staying in the house. Surely Carson didn't take care of this whole place by himself. No, of course not, it was impossible. One man alone…

She stamped the snow off her boots and went into the warm, clean kitchen. She'd even shined the copper pots and hung them on a rack near the stove. With the cabinets redone and some of that no-wax vinyl flooring replacing the old linoleum, the place would look great. Loosely woven curtains of thick yarn would add just the right home-spun look…soft yellow and sky blue, a subtle touch of pink running through them. She'd seen the material at the dry-goods store last time she went to town.

After checking the dumplings, she warmed a can of peas and carrots. For dessert, she made short bread and heated a can of applesauce with butter and cinnamon. That was all she could find. Tomorrow she'd go home and bring over some meat and things.

Sighing, she put on a fresh pot of coffee and sat down to wait for her fate to come walking in. It was getting late. Where was he?

Carson drove the empty truck along the treacherous gravel road toward the house. He'd delivered the last load of carcasses—his year's profit—to the dealer. There'd be no increase in the herd this year. He'd have to sell off every calf that had made it to pay his taxes and the interest on the loan.

"Damn," he muttered as the truck hit a pothole and he bounced against the roof. As soon as the weather cleared, he needed to grade the road. Let's see, that would be chore number one thousand ten on his list of things to do. He managed a feeble grin.

When he turned the last bend in the road, he blinked. A light was on in the house. At the back. He must have turned it on at noon and forgotten to turn it off. He was slipping. Electricity cost money. He was careful with that scarce commodity.

He parked the truck in the equipment barn and headed straight for the stable. He had stock to care for.

A few minutes later he studied the horses, totally perplexed. The stables were clean, the animals bedded down already. He peered in the mangers. A few pieces of cracked corn and oats. Fresh water in the buckets. The hair rose on his neck.

Either the good fairy had come to visit or someone was in his house. He strode grimly toward the dwelling, but came to an abrupt halt halfway across the clearing between the house and outbuildings.

Through the deepening dusk, he spied a red Mustang parked behind the house. It couldn't be. It was.

Just what was she doing here?

He stomped the snow and mud off his boots and entered the kitchen. A figure in a red sweater and jeans—a very feminine figure—stood in front of the stove.

"About time you got in," Tess said, stirring the soup. "Where have you been until all hours?"

"What," Carson bit out, "in the hell are you doing here?"

"Working."

He removed his coat and hat and tossed them on a hook behind the door. Sitting on a parson's bench, he tugged off his boots and stored them inside the bench.

On stockinged feet, he strode across the room, looking like the Wrath of God, she thought. He grabbed her wrist, wrestled the spoon out of her hand, threw it down on the clean stove and hauled her around to face him.

"No games, Tess," he warned. "Why are you here?"

She smiled triumphantly. "Just as I said—working. I'm your new partner."

"You're not," he said.

"I am."

She returned his glare with a composure she was far from feeling. Any minute now he was going to move his hands from her wrists to her throat. *"She died so young," everyone will say,* she thought inanely. *Send red roses.*

"What?" he snapped at her. "What did you say?"

"Send roses for my funeral. They're my favorite flower." She smiled impudently at him, even though she was shaking inside.

Her quip made him even angrier, if that was possible. He gave her a little shake. "Tell me what you're doing here...now!" he thundered, his eyes flashing lightning bolts.

"I'll explain, just as soon as you release me so I can get supper on the table," she said, being reasonable. "Wash up."

For a second she didn't think he was going to obey her order, however, after giving her one more fulminating glance, he stalked off. "This had better be good," he muttered.

Tess set the table with Fiesta dishes, giving Carson a matching place setting of teal blue and choosing the red for herself. She had found a sunny yellow tablecloth and put it on the table earlier. The napkins matched the dinnerware.

She poured glasses of milk for each of them and was just placing them on the table when Carson reappeared, his hands and face washed, his curly hair combed into order.

"It's ready," she announced unnecessarily. Now that the moment for explanation was at hand, she didn't feel quite as brave as she had when the confrontation was in the offing.

The two bowls of food, although large, looked rather meager on a table that could easily accommodate eight large men and all the fixings of a feast.

"It's not much," she began, then remembered it was all she'd found in his pantry. There had been a small amount of mushy soup in the pot before she washed it to stew the chicken. "I didn't make any bread. Because of the dumplings."

"This is fine."

His voice sounded rough, as if he had a hard time getting the words out. He handed her the bowl of chicken and dumplings and waited until she had served herself before taking a portion. Then they began the silent meal.

After she finished, Tess watched him. He didn't gobble the food, but he did eat steadily, until both bowls were empty. He wiped his mouth on the napkin. "God, that was good."

"I'm glad you enjoyed it," she said, a big, silly grin on her face. He liked her cooking!

A flush spread up Carson's neck and onto his ears. He gave a short laugh. "Anything would taste good after weeks of soup."

He saw the brief hurt flicker into her eyes and wished he had let the compliment stand. But it was better to hurt her now than later. He'd squash the attraction between them once and for all. That had been his reasoning when she was seventeen. It still seemed appropriate five years later.

"I think it's time we had our little talk and straightened out this nonsense," he said.

"It isn't nonsense." She stood and cleared the table. After splitting pieces of short bread in half and placing them in clean bowls, she spooned the warm applesauce over them and put them on the table. "Dessert," she announced, taking her chair once more.

He glared at her, then the food, but he ate it. He hadn't had anything half so good in years.

"Coffee in the living room? A fire would be nice," she suggested. "Go ahead. I'll be along in a moment."

He knew the house was cold and drafty in spite of the efforts of the gas furnace that had been installed under the sprawling ranch house in the early days of his parents' marriage. The walls and attic needed insulating. So what else was new? He went into the living room as ordered.

The fire was warming the cold room by the time Tess entered carrying two coffee cups. Carson rose from the hearth and took one from her. She smiled, and his heart felt lighter.

Don't be stupid, he snarled at himself. He resumed his place on the stone hearth after she sat on the sofa. "Now. Tell me what you think you're doing," he demanded, taking things in hand.

"I told you—working. As your partner—"

"Dammit, you're not my partner. I don't have a partner. And I don't want one," he added, seeing the argument forming on her lips. He took a sip of coffee. He couldn't stop the surprise from showing on his face.

"Mocha mint," she said, obviously pleased with herself. "I added some cocoa and mint oil I found in the pantry. Your coffee had gone stale and lost most of its flavor. You should keep it in the freezer part of the refrigerator."

"Tess," he warned, feeling the bounds on his temper loosening. When she looked at him like that, he wanted to...

Never mind what he wanted to do. "I want you to go home and quit playing games. I'm not in the mood for them." He ran a hand through his hair, ruining the careful brushing he'd given it before dinner. "I don't want to hurt you, but...I might."

There, he had given her warning. If she pushed him

too far, he just might lose control. If that happened, he'd take her, right there on the hard floor in front of the fire, the way he had once dreamed it. Only then, he had thought to have candlelight and wine. A soft comforter to lay her on. A whole new world to discover as he undressed her.

"What's wrong?" she asked, her voice tender with concern.

He blinked and looked away, staring into the fire until his blood quit rioting through his body. "Nothing," he said. "Just tired." He glanced at her, "Tell me," he said, part order, part request.

Tess faced her moment of truth, as her literature professor would have said. "I opened your letter to my sister." She paused for an explosion. None came. "Then I checked the safe and found your loan papers. So I called Lainie and bought the I.O.U. I think I own about one-fifth of this ranch now."

Carson watched her as she made her explanation, her manner so reasonable and cool, butter wouldn't have melted on her tongue. She was calm on the outside, but was her stomach giving her fits? Did she hurt?

He pushed the thought away. He had no time for gentleness in his life. Tess was a complication he couldn't handle. There were too many other problems demanding his time and attention.

"All right, so I owe you instead of your sister," he said when she finished. "That fact doesn't make you a partner. I'm not going to be able to make a payment on the principle this year. If you want the place, you can foreclose."

"What would I do with it?" She gestured impatiently, her shoulders lifting under the red sweater, making her breasts jiggle. Wasn't she wearing any underclothes? He almost groaned aloud as a shaft of desire raced through him.

"Add it to the Garrick acres," he said. His voice came out harsher than he'd intended as he fought the passion she induced.

Tess looked away from him and stared into the fire while she sipped the flavored coffee. No flicker of emotion appeared on her oval face. She had herself under control.

"What about your dream?" she asked softly. She turned the full force of those honey-brown eyes on him. "What about your plans to make this into a thriving ranch again?"

"They came up against the brick wall called life and broke," he answered, anger and need battling for supremacy in him.

To hold her, to be held, to let her comfort him. Damn, but he was going soft just being around her for an hour. In another minute he'd have to be picked up off the floor like a wet noodle.

"Get on home, Tess Garrick. I haven't time for your games anymore," he told her with a smile, trying to be easy with her. He didn't want to hurt her. God knows, he'd never wanted that.

She shook her head.

He didn't need a lot of insight to recognize stubbornness in every inch of her delectable body.

"I'm here to check out your operation," she informed him. "In business circles, that's known as 'protecting your investment.'"

"What do you know about business—or a working ranch for that matter?" he added as an afterthought.

She was on her feet in an instant, hands on hips. "What do I know? I happen to have a degree in business management. You may recall that you told me I was a green kid, that I should get some schooling so I'd know what was what. Well, I have. I intend to use it...right here!" She flung herself on the sofa again.

It was Carson's turn to pace the floor between the coffee table and the couch. "All right, so you have a vested interest. You can't stay here alone with me. People will talk. Your family won't allow it."

She raised her eyebrows loftily. "How can they stop me? I'm of age and sound mind."

"Sure about the last one?"

"Yes."

They stared at each other, neither willing to give. He turned and, needing something to do, added another log to the blazing fire. "So," he said, taking a soft approach to catch her off guard, "you're going to join me as my partner. Well, maybe that won't be so bad. Supper sure was good tonight."

"Thank you," she said.

"I'd expect something like that every night."

"Okay."

Hmm, he thought. That wasn't the reaction he'd expected. Tess was a modern woman, liberated and all that. "And, of course, there's the house. You'd have to keep it neat."

"It'll be a lot cleaner than what I saw of your efforts,'' she said, a little smirk curling her lips up at the edges.

He imagined nibbling on them until she opened her mouth to him and kissed him with all the passion in her. Whoa right there, stupid. That isn't part of the plan. He cast about for something else to discourage her.

''I used to see you working with the horses in the summer at your place. I think you should take over their care.''

''Are those five in the stable all you've got?''

''There's a couple of mares someplace on the range. They ran off with a wild stallion before Christmas.''

Was that why she was here? he questioned. Was the call of the blood stronger than common sense? Maybe she was reacting to nature and its prodding. Once she had wanted him with a wild passion.

''Five, six, seven horses, they'll be a snap compared to the number at our place,'' she said. ''I see no problem.''

''I'm aware of the size and success of the Garrick ranch,'' Carson said. Damn her, she would have to bring her family ranch into the discussion. It made him that much more aware of his own failure. He'd once told her he would make the McCumber spread into one her brother would envy. Ha! The stupid things a man will say when he's young and thinks he's in love.

''I didn't mean to sound condescending.'' She paused and considered. ''But I guess I did. I apologize, Carson.'' A slow smile brightened her face.

"We can make this into the best ranch in three valleys," she promised.

"There is no *we*," he snapped.

"Of course there is." She stood, stretched and yawned. "Well, I'd better get the kitchen cleaned up or the boss will chew me out. Then I think I'll head on to bed. I took the guest room with the cabbage roses."

She walked out, leaving him standing there thinking of bowers of roses and beds made up with red silk sheets.

Chapter Three

So far, so good, Tess assured herself the next morning. She sat in the warm sun that streamed through the kitchen windows, basking like a contented cat. But not too contented. Just because Carson had given up the argument last night didn't mean he would today. She knew how changeable men could be.

The timer on the dryer buzzed.

At a brisk pace, she went into the large pantry next to the kitchen and removed the sheets from the tumbler. The day was going well enough. When her alarm went off at five, she had jumped out of bed, raring to get started. Since then, she'd washed the linens stored in the big closet next to the washer and dryer, the ones off Carson's bed and the set she'd found in his closet.

For just the briefest instant, she allowed herself to daydream of waking in the same bed with him, her cologne mingling with his after-shave, the intimate scent of lovemaking surrounding them.

Her fantasy stirred the wildest impulses within her. She wanted to find him, to throw herself into his arms, to... With a heartfelt sigh she blinked the vision away. First things first.

Food was the most pressing necessity. She planned to go over to the ranch and bring back a carload of meat and vegetables. While surveying the cabinets, refrigerator and freezer, she'd found enough staples such as flour and sugar, but not much else.

Speaking of food, she wondered if Carson had eaten any breakfast. He'd left the house before she got up and had gone off without a trace—no used plate or bowl in the sink, no coffee in the pot. Apparently he intended to ignore her until she gave up.

Well, let him be stubborn. She had a good bit of that trait herself. They'd see who outlasted the other.

After folding the last set of sweet-smelling linens and putting them away, she got her list, started her car and headed for the ridge road. The ground was still frozen, so she should be able to get over and back with no trouble. However, the way the sun was shining, they were in for a fast spring thaw. That could be dangerous. Flash floods would fill the many channels that cut through the rugged land. She pressed on the accelerator and drove faster over the crusty snow and hard-packed gravel.

Two hours later she returned, the trunk and back seat of the small car loaded with foodstuffs fit to grace a king's table. It was well past time for lunch. Her stomach growled.

Where was Carson?

If he didn't come in for lunch, they were going to have round two of their private battle when she did see him. She planned the scathing things she would say to him as she put packages of meat into the freezer.

Her temper rose as she mentally rehearsed the volatile scene. At last, thoroughly angry, she flung bags of fruit and vegetables into the three freezer baskets. When one broke open, spilling luscious strawberries into the interior, she blamed Carson, then realized the futility of her actions. With a wry grimace, she picked up the berries, found another bag and proceeded in a more orderly fashion. In a short time, she had all the boxes and bags unpacked and the food stored.

Mason jars filled with tomatoes—whole, juiced or pureed—corn, salsa, piccalilli, green beans and other produce gleamed from the pantry shelves in jewel tones of red, yellow and green like a secret treasure. Tess smiled, pleased with her bounty.

Removing a package of ham, already cured and sliced into sandwich meat, she returned to the kitchen and placed the ham in the microwave oven to thaw.

What would Carson say about the new appliance? Tess had requested the microwave for Christmas during her first year in college. It had proved a timesaver and she'd grown accustomed to using it. So now it was installed on the underside of the cabinet in Carson's kitchen.

She'd also brought an old Klaxon horn, formerly used for cheering the home team during football and basketball games. She had another purpose in mind.

After making thick sandwiches of pepper ham with lettuce and tomato, served with chips, pickles and a plate of fresh vegetables, she opened the back door and stuck the horn out.

The noise of the Klaxon intruded on the silent ranch like St. Peter's trumpet on Judgment Day. The sound rolled over the hills, reverberated against the limestone ridge and echoed back. It even made Tess jump. The horses threw up their heads and raced around the paddock like Thoroughbreds at Belmont.

After giving several toots, Tess withdrew into the house. That should bring some results.

It did.

Carson rode into the stable yard fifteen minutes later. His horse was lathered, but he didn't stop to unsaddle or rub it down. With one lithe swing of his leg over the pommel, he was on the ground and running toward the house. He burst into the kitchen.

"Lunch," Tess announced, smiling over her shoulder as she placed their plates on the table.

Carson's expression was a comic study in disbelief. "You called me in for lunch?" he asked, panting from his wild trip.

"Yes, it's after two o'clock." She was extremely reasonable and calm.

"You blew some damned horn—"

"A Klaxon. From school," she added, feeling the need to explain. Carson now resembled an Arizona thundercloud, rolling down from the mountains, black as sin and twice as mean, as Zed was sometimes heard to say.

"I know what the damned thing is," he roared, his temper exploding as he realized she was all right.

Tess had expected the reaction. Men were really quite predictable. Food would calm the beast. She hoped.

"Have you washed your hands?" she asked.

"Do you realize what I thought...what I went through getting here? I nearly ruined my best horse... I thought you were hurt..."

Words seemed to fail him. Tess felt a surge of adrenaline as she watched him clench his fists. Should she run? No, she'd thought it out. Confrontation was the only way.

She whirled on him, hands on hips, fury suddenly spitting from her eyes. "And I thought you were either starved or frozen to death. What time did you leave this morning? Why didn't you wait for breakfast? I told you I'd tend the stable horses. Why didn't you leave them to me? There's a notepad by the telephone. Why didn't you let me know where you were working and what time to expect you in? That's the first rule on any ranch, that you keep everyone informed of your whereabouts—"

"I don't recall agreeing to report in to you," he interrupted, his gaze going cold as hoarfrost.

She glared right back. Lifting her head haughtily, she replied, "It's only common courtesy to let your partner know—"

"I told you you're not my partner! We went through that last night. I want you out of here. Pronto!" He took a menacing step toward her.

"Take off your boots," she said, reverting to a

calm manner. "I mopped this floor yesterday for an hour to get it clean."

For a tense five seconds she thought he was going to take her by the collar and toss her out into the snow, but after what she sensed was an internal battle, he stomped over to the bench and removed his muddy boots. "This isn't going to work," he warned.

"Our partnership?" she asked. "Beer, soda, milk, iced tea?"

"Milk. Where'd the beer come from? I don't drink and I don't keep liquor in the house."

"Sorry. I'll get rid of it next time I go over to the other ranch. Is it because of your father, your not drinking and all?"

"That's none of your business."

She sighed loudly. "Of course it's my business. I have an interest in this place—"

"Which gives you no rights whatsoever to my private life." He frowned. "Or even to my business one. The loan only covers about a tenth of the ranch."

"Oh. I thought I owned about a fifth." She was disappointed it wasn't more. The more indebted he was to her, the more clout she felt she had.

"Legally, you have no right to come in and take over—"

"You agreed last night to my being here. Remember? Cooking, cleaning, tending the horses, those were my assigned chores. I can keep the books, too. I'm really good at that."

"I'll bet," he muttered.

"I am," she assured him, taking an innocent tone as if she hadn't noticed the sarcasm in his voice.

Carson took a deep breath, let it out slowly. He looked resigned to his fate. Tess considered that a good omen.

"Let's eat. I have work to do. Where's the milk?"

"Isn't *please* in your vocabulary?"

"Maybe," he said. His sudden grin was mocking.

She poured him a big glass, thought for a moment, and then poured one for herself. Milk could cause acid rebound, but her stomach hadn't bothered her for days...in spite of her quarrels with the unmanageable male at the table.

Taking her seat across from him, she cast him a glance of exasperation. He was trying to throw her off track by changing his tactics, which was the strategy she'd decided to use on him. Time would declare the winner.

"Besides, why should I say please?" he continued. "This is your job, remember?" He sounded entirely reasonable.

"I'm your partner, not your slave," she said, picking up her sandwich. She realized she was starving and took a big bite.

Carson did the same. He ate just as he had last night, steadily until every crumb was gone. When he finished, she brought out a pie and cut him a large slice.

"Chess," he said in an odd tone. "I haven't had chess pie since...since my mother died."

"Rose had made four for our hands. I stole one. Zed and the boys could stand to lose a couple of pounds."

"You brought this stuff from the Garrick ranch?" Carson asked, his face hardening.

Tess glanced at him warily. "Of course. Did you think I conjured it out of thin air?"

"I assumed you went to the grocery in town. Figure up how much this would have cost. I'll pay you back."

"No charge," she said, waving his offer aside. "This is my contribution to—"

He shoved away from the table without tasting the pie. "I said figure up the cost. When you get tired of playing your little game, I don't intend to be indebted to you any more than I am right now." He jerked on his boots and left, slamming the door with a bang as startling as the Klaxon had been.

"This is no game," she said, but only the tick of the clock answered her. She put the pie away.

"Ohhh," Tess groaned. She pressed her hands to the small of her back. During her years at college she'd forgotten how tiring vacuuming could be. Cleaning up a single room containing a bed, dresser and desk was a lot less work than cleaning a ranch house with a huge living room, office, kitchen, pantry, three bedrooms, two full-sized bathrooms and a smaller room that could be used as a sewing room or nursery. It had both types of furniture in it.

She glanced out the window. The sun had been bright again today, and the snow was melting fast. Flash-flood warnings were out all over the state. She chewed on her lower lip.

Where was Carson?

Again he'd left the house before she got up, even though she'd set her clock for four-thirty that morning. This one-upmanship was getting ridiculous. Soon they'd be starting the new day before the old was over.

After putting the vacuum cleaner, dust rags and cleaning paraphernalia in the storage closet, she took a slow walk through the house. It was spotless. Every oak, maple, cherry or walnut surface gleamed with the soft patina produced by age and the polishing cloth. She stopped before the gun case.

Hunting rifles and shotguns were neatly lined up behind the locked glass doors. Ancient dueling pistols, plated with gold-and-silver filigree on the handles, resided in a velvet case. The workmanship was beautiful. Carson could have sold those for a lot of money.

So there remained a vein of sentimentality in his flinty demeanor after all, she mused. It was encouraging to know he still had a softer side. If she could only reach it.

She continued on her journey through the silent house. The faint musty odor was gone. The scent of lemon oil from the polish permeated the air. When she opened Carson's closet, disclosing rows of freshly laundered shirts and work clothes, the delicious scent of cloves and cinnamon wafted around her, teasing her nostrils. She'd put sachets of spices in every closet.

Her favorite hang-up sachets were drying in front of the hot-air register on the kitchen floor. She'd mixed unsweetened applesauce with ground cinnamon until the batter was thick enough to cut into interesting shapes with cookie cutters. Then she'd pressed a piece of yarn into each so it could be tied to a clothes rack or nail. Her mother had taught her how to make them.

Tears filmed her eyes. She wished she could talk to her mother about life and love and all the problems that seemed to go with them. She could call her sister, but Dev wanted Lainie to have complete rest, and she'd already bothered Lainie with ranch business. No, this was one time she was going to have to stand on her own without the Garrick family behind her.

But what about the Garrick money?

More specifically, what about her money that had been banked for her since her parents' deaths? She had a lot now. The amount she'd paid for Carson's note wasn't half of what she had in money-market and mutual funds.

Well, she'd think about that later. It was time for supper. Carson hadn't come in for lunch even though she'd blasted the darned Klaxon until her ears rang. Going into the kitchen, she put on a pot of coffee and checked on the roast chicken. It was done to the point of falling apart. Savory dressing was browned to perfection. Mashed potatoes and green beans waited to be spooned into bowls. Salads were in the refrigerator.

Tess opened the back door and stepped out on the great slab of stone almost large enough to be a patio. Although the last two days had been warm, the air was far from balmy. When the sun sank below the horizon, the temperature dropped into the freezing range again.

The paddocks were muddy and the south slopes of the hills bare, but there was plenty of snow on the shaded sides of the mountains and under the trees. She could hear the threatening mumble of little rivulets running into depressions and gullies, following the lay of the land to the creek. There'd be flood waters by tomorrow in all the dry washes.

The horses were already in their stalls, fed, watered and bedded down. She heard some nervous whickers from that direction. What was bothering them?

The trumpeting call of a horse answered her. Glancing up, she saw a magnificent wild stallion on the ridge.

He reared up and pawed the air. His coloring was the striking combination of the Appaloosa. White was dominant on most of his body with a few brown spots, but it changed to brown with white spots on his rump. The last flaring rays of the sun caught him as he challenged all comers, turning him the color of rose gold.

Tess felt the stirring of her own spirit, as if it wanted to accept the mustang's challenge. She stared, spellbound, feeling the indescribable call of the wild that Jack London had written about. A great yearning seized her heart.

The sound of the pickup truck sent the stallion charging off the hill and out of sight. She turned and watched Carson drive up and park. He climbed out without acknowledging her presence and headed toward the stable.

Something in his manner alerted her. When she glimpsed his bandanna wrapped around his hand, she went in and changed to her boots. When she entered the stable a few minutes later, she heard him in the tack room. The strong scent of liniment filled the air. She walked to the open door, worry eating her insides. For the first time in more than a week, her stomach tensed.

He was pouring the medicine over his hand.

"Let me see," she exclaimed, going to him.

Carson turned his shoulder to her. "It's nothing."

"Fine," she said dryly. "Let me see it."

She moved in front of him and grabbed his arm before he could turn away again. A gash ran from the base of his finger to the thick pad of his thumb on his left hand. It was deep and bloody, but looked clean.

"How did you do that?" she demanded.

"On some old barbed wire. A cow had gotten entangled in it. Damned stupid animal. If she'd held still until I got her free, we'd both have been all right."

He cursed some more when Tess found the iodine and poured it over the wound. After attaching butterfly bandages across the cut, she took the gauze from the medicine chest and began methodically wrapping his hand.

"You'll need to rest this for a few days until it heals," she advised, putting the medicines and gauze away. "Supper's ready. Where were you at lunch? I blew the horn for you to come in."

"I was busy," he said, his voice clipped.

"You need some help around here—"

"Don't start," he warned. "I'm in no mood for an argument."

She led the way to the house. Once inside, she motioned for him to sit on the bench. Pushing his hands aside impatiently, she yanked his boots off none too gently. He stood up and watched her as she pulled her own off and stored both pairs on the rack cleverly built inside the seat.

"Come on. I'll help you wash up." She led the way to the big sink in the pantry.

"I can handle it."

"You don't want to get that bandage wet. I'd have to put on another, and I'm not sure we have any gauze in the house."

Going into the pantry, she realized she was angry at him for getting hurt and also for not coming in at lunch. And for not having breakfast with her. Or being glad to see her. Her list was growing long, and she'd only been there for two days.

She squeezed soap into her hands and rubbed it into a lather. "Give me your hand," she ordered.

He did so, careful not to touch her side as he slid his arm in front of her and over the sink. She washed his hand and forearm with brisk, scrubbing motions. She glanced at his face.

"You have mud on your cheek. I'll wash it, too."

She got a washcloth from the fresh stack in the closet and proceeded to wash his face as if he were her four-year-old nephew. Except his skin was rough with beard. Little lines were forming at the corners of his eyes from his days in the sun. His forehead was whiter than his jaw because of his hat.

A man's face, she thought, rubbing the streaks off with the soapy rag. Her anger dissolved and was replaced by a great tenderness. For all that he was a man, she felt he needed the secure blanket of love around him perhaps even more than Davie did. Deep inside, she knew Carson hadn't had enough of just pure, simple loving in his life.

She ached to give him her love, to slather him with it so that his heart and soul could open up to her. Was he afraid of love, afraid of getting hurt if he let himself be vulnerable? It was a chance everyone had to take sooner or later.

"Close your eyes," she said softly.

She rinsed the soap from his face, starting with his eyelids. She wiped the lather off his forehead and nose, his cheeks and mouth. At last she lingered on his hard jawline, letting the cloth flow over it and down his neck.

He opened his eyes and captured hers. All the longing she felt for him was in their depths. She didn't try to hide it. She couldn't.

The powerful muscles in his neck jerked under her hands. Without pausing to think, she dropped the cloth into the sink and cupped his face between her palms, holding him gently...so gently.

His eyes seemed to get even darker, and she was lost in them. "Carson," she whispered. The wildness bloomed in her, longing for appeasement. If he would only touch her....

The moment hung suspended in time. Tess tried to connect with him, to feel they were on the same wavelength. She witnessed emotion in him, but not any she could recognize. He displayed no yearning for her, not even hunger for sexual satisfaction. There were only shadows, and those she couldn't read.

Finally, unable to bear the tension any longer, she let him go and stepped back. Loneliness washed over her. She'd felt it before: every night she'd been away from home had seemed endless.

"Something smells good," he commented suddenly. He sniffed the air. "In fact, everything does."

"Lemon oil," she said, smiling past the sadness she felt as she went into the kitchen to set the table. "Cloves, cinnamon." She removed the chicken from the oven and placed it on a trivet. "Sage and onions and garlic."

"Enough," Carson growled. "I'm starving."

"Then sit."

He did. She dished everything up. When she sat across from him, she noticed the last of the sunset was gone. The sky was lavender and purple, fading to navy blue in the east. The stallion stood on the ridge again, his head held at an alert angle as he stared at the dwellings below. Two mares came up beside the stallion.

"Carson, look," Tess whispered as if the animals would hear and take fright. "The stallion and his family. There he is with two of his mares."

"*My* mares," Carson said, leaping up from the table. "Maybe I can get them back."

Tess was after him in an instant. "No!" She grabbed his arm and held on, stopping him.

"What the hell...?" he snapped, trying to pull

away from her grasp. Pain flushed across his handsome face as he used his left hand.

"Be careful with your hand," she admonished. "Let the stallion keep his little herd for a while. The ground is too wet for the truck, and nothing else on the ranch can outrun him. Let him go for now."

Carson frowned at her, determination written large in his harsh gaze, but at least he acknowledged the wisdom of her advice. "All right. But I'll get them back and I'll run him clear out of the country," he averred.

"I'm sure you will." She urged him back to the table, and they ate the savory meal in silence. After finishing, she sent him into the living room to light the fire she had laid earlier.

She cleaned the kitchen, then transferred slices of pie and mugs of steaming coffee to a tray. Carrying them into the other room, she went over her earlier plans to talk him into hiring some help for the ranch. He'd never get anywhere working alone.

She took a seat on the sofa. He moved away from the fire and sat on the opposite end. Silence filled the room while they ate the dessert. When she started to take the tray to the kitchen, he stood and took it from her.

"You've done enough today," he said.

Tess kicked off her shoes and drew her legs up. She leaned into the corner and let her lashes drift low over her eyes. The flames coalesced into a golden crystal with lines radiating to the farthest edges of her vision. Dreams came to her, borne on a magic carpet woven of fire.

* * *

Carson strode into the room, his footfalls making no sound on the rug. Tess lay on the sofa, one arm behind her head, the other across her waist. Her breasts jutted against the knitted fabric of her sweater. Tonight she wore a gold one with her jeans.

She was tall, slender and splendidly proportioned, a country goddess in her casual clothes, beautiful but not rustic. She'd never be that. She was Tess Garrick, heiress. She'd been to Europe during the summer between her junior and senior year. He'd read all about it in the local paper. And dreamed of discovering ancient statues and gardens with her for months afterward.

He forced himself away from the memory. He had no time for thoughts like that. Turning from her, he roamed around the room, his glance taking in every detail of work she'd done.

The whole house was shiny and clean. It had smelled like heaven when he walked into the kitchen after a day of hard work. He'd moved his small herd to higher ground in anticipation of the floods he knew were coming. The county road would be closed by dawn tomorrow. The ridge road was already impassable.

He stopped his pacing at the end of the sofa and looked his fill at Tess. Did she realize they were stranded here together?

As he watched, she moved, stretching one leg out straight, leaving the other crooked at the knee, the sole of her foot against her leg. He stared at the triangle thus formed.

Slowly his gaze went to the apex of that triangle.

The sweet secret of her womanhood called to him. The blood stirred painfully in all his manly parts, answering that call. Five years and he'd never wanted another woman.

It was insane to want Tess Garrick.

What did he have to offer her? He counted his assets on one hand: a house that needed major work, a rundown ranch that was going nowhere, a few horses, a scraggly herd of cows and himself.

His mouth curled sardonically. Yeah, he was a real prize catch for the rich Miss Garrick of the Garrick Valley Ranch.

He pivoted on one foot and walked away, but after stoking up the fire, he couldn't stop from turning toward her again.

Her mouth was gentle, its lines all lovely curves. The bottom lip was just a tad fuller than the upper one. The indentation below her nose was seductively deep, rising to twin crests that connected to her upper lip. She was made for kissing.

Against his will, he was drawn to her. All the longings that he had buried burst from the solitary confinement he'd imposed on himself for five long years. He sat on the sofa beside her and let his eyes make love to her.

He didn't know how long he stared, drinking in the sight of her loveliness like a man who'd been stranded in a desert for years. All at once he was aware of her eyes, golden in the firelight, looking at him.

He groaned aloud, hearing the sound as an admission of defeat. God, how he wanted her. Before he could stand and make his escape, she reached for him.

He was lost.

Her hands closed over his shoulders, tugging him to her. Her radiant smile, the warmth of her body, the scent that was hers caressed his senses with a thousand pinpricks of desire.

"Carson," she murmured. Entreaty seeped from her lips with a sigh. He had to answer. To resist the slumberous beauty of her was more than he could do.

"Tess, tell me to go away," he ordered, his voice hoarse with effort. He'd die if she did.

She shook her head. The firelight flickered through the golden-brown waves spread over her shoulders. He reached for a curl and rubbed it between his finger and thumb. She again pulled on him, inviting him into her embrace. Heaven awaited him there. He had experienced it once in his life and had never forgotten.

"Kiss me, Carson," she said. "I've waited so long."

He raised a hand to her face. His fingers trembled slightly, he noticed. He hoped she didn't. She'd think him a clumsy fool.

With the gentlest caress he was capable of, he stroked along her cheek. As her hands tightened, he let himself be pulled downward until they were no more than an inch apart.

He lowered his head, and their mouths touched briefly. Staring into her eyes, he let himself drift upon the golden sea of her desire. She was a woman now, not a child, and she was looking at him with a woman's passion. His body quickened. He wanted to be in her, to feel the warm welcome of her body to his.

Her hands slipped into his hair and she drew his mouth to hers again. The contact deepened. He opened his mouth, wanting her with an urgent hunger that recognized no other need at the moment. To hell with tomorrow. He'd take tonight.

Without losing contact, he shifted his position to lie beside her. Her breasts prodded his chest. Her abdomen and thighs pressed lightly against his. He slipped one arm under her head, the other around her small waist.

She seemed incredibly delicate to him. A need to be gentle joined with the hunger, fusing them into one sweet clove of passion.

"Touch me," she whispered, running her hand through his hair.

He caressed her back, her sides and the sweeping curve of her hip. On the return trip, he moved upward and rested his hand just below her breast. She made an impatient sound, a kitten mew of demand that pleased him.

"If I do," he warned, "there may be no turning back."

"Good," she said.

For another heartbeat he hesitated, then he let his hand glide over the burgeoning mound and cup the full flesh of her breast. A red haze gathered behind his closed eyes as he felt her nipple meet the palm of his hand.

She wanted him. He wanted her. Sex between a

man and a woman was simple enough. Why did it always seem like more between them?

Carson tried not to think of the complications of making love to Tess, but they intruded into the fog that surrounded them. Soon she'd tire of her game and run back home where a housekeeper cooked all the meals and cleaned the house, where fifty cowhands cleaned the stables of the ranch stock and the show horses they raised.

What did it matter? He'd take tonight.

With savage urgency, he probed her mouth with his tongue, devouring the honey he found there. When she answered with an equal amount of intensity, he forgot everything but the contact of her flesh against his. His body strained against his jeans. He shifted slightly, and the hardness pressed against her. He heard her quick intake of breath and felt the movement of her hips against him as she responded.

"Tonight," he murmured. "I'll take tonight."

Chapter Four

Tess fought to maintain the sweet haze of passion that shut her off from reality. She wanted only the sensation of his lips and hands on her, the pleasure of his body pressed so warmly to her own. She didn't want to think.

But his words intruded. *Tonight. I'll take tonight.* It wasn't enough. She was here to fight for their future, for all the nights to come in a long and happy union that was more than passion. Some instinct warned her against letting the heat of the moment wipe out the promise of tomorrow.

Gently she stroked the back of his neck, loving the feel of his short hair against her fingers and wishing she and Carson could stay like that forever. She turned her head, freeing her mouth from his rapacious hunger, tears suddenly near the surface. Men hated woman who led them on.

When he bent his attention on her neck, kissing and nuzzling the sensitive skin, she nearly forgot the inner warning and took what was available. With a sigh, she exerted control over her wayward emotions and began to the task of calming his.

With the softest touch, she slipped her hands between them and pressed her palms against his cheek. He responded automatically to that pressure, easing his body from hers slightly. When she pressed more, he retreated farther until a space was created between them. He lifted his head and gazed down at her.

Slowly the passion receded as he recognized the refusal in her smile. "I'd never have taken you for a tease," he said.

"The time isn't right." She had to have his love—his freely given love—before she gave herself. If he took her, then felt he had to marry her, she wouldn't be able to bear the pain.

He looked puzzled, then a light dawned in his eyes. "A bad time of the moon—"

She shook her head. "Not that. The time isn't right for us. I want more than a night of bliss." Should she tell him exactly what she did want? At moments like this, when she wanted him the most, she was too vulnerable to open herself that much.

He levered himself up and away from her. When he stood, she sat upright and smoothed her hair with trembly fingers.

"There's nothing more," he informed her coldly. "I have nothing else to give you."

"There used to be," she insisted. "That summer

you worked at the ranch, there was more. We shared thoughts and dreams.''

He laughed and ran a hand through his mussed hair. ''You're still a kid if you think what happened five years ago between us was more than the natural functioning of hormones and proximity.'' He stared out the darkened window. With evident reluctance, he added, ''And maybe a dollop of imagination.''

It soothed her that he admitted to even something as elusive as imagination. ''I loved you. I think you loved me.''

''If you have to believe that to make you feel better about the whole stupid episode, be my guest.''

Tess felt the hurt spiral inside her like a pinwheel in which all the lines seem to run toward the middle. Refusing to be defeated, she challenged, ''Are you afraid of falling in love?''

''No,'' he said. ''I just look at life from a more practical viewpoint than the one of sweetness and light you seem to see. You've had it easy, Tess. Heaven knows I don't want to be the one to disillusion you, but you give me no choice. If you stay here, you'll get a dose of real life, unvarnished by the Garrick name and money. You might get more than you bargained for,'' he warned. ''I want you, I can't deny that, but it would be sex, nothing more. Do you understand?''

She nodded. ''Is that why you're telling me all this?'' A tiny smiled played around the corners of her mouth.

''Don't read some noble sentiment into it. I believe in playing fair, that's all.''

"Well, then," she said with great practicality, "warning has been given and accepted. I'm tired. Tomorrow I'm going to round up the chickens I saw in the stable and shed and put them in the hen house. Will you have time to repair the roof? It leaks in one corner. Oh, I'll need some money for chicken feed." She looked at him expectantly.

He shook his head as if trying to clear it of other thoughts. "I'll write you a check for it, and for the groceries."

"Thanks." With a show of poise, she jumped up from the sofa, glanced once with longing at the fire, then hustled herself off to bed. Now that she knew he had fresher memories to put with the old ones, she would back off and let the pot simmer, so to speak.

Carson was in the kitchen when Tess went in the next morning. She couldn't disguise her start of surprise at finding him still there. "Here. Here's some money," he said, shoving a check across the table.

She glanced at it. "Two hundred's too much. A hundred will take care of everything."

"You might need to pick up a few other items when you go to town. The roads should be open tomorrow or the next day."

"Good idea. There's some material at the dry-goods store. I'm thinking of making curtains for in here."

He made a gruff sound that she decided to take as agreement. Although he looked as tough as a long-horned bull, she was elated. Score one for my side, she thought, but was careful to keep the glee off her face.

Going to the stove, she noted he had only coffee in front of him. There was no sign of breakfast. Without asking, she cooked bacon in the microwave and made a big pot of oatmeal. She placed the food on the table along with whole-wheat toast and jelly.

"You didn't have to do that," he told her. He looked at her, his gaze level and impersonal, as if last night had never happened. "I don't really expect you to cook for me."

"I don't mind. It's part of the bargain." She smiled perkily at him while watching the cool control slip from his eyes and be replaced with smoldering anger.

He finished the meal and stood. "I'll be working on the hen house."

She didn't dare comment, not after the harsh look he gave her before pulling on his boots and stomping out. Going to a window, she watched him disappear around the stable, then checked the sky. The day promised to be another bright and fair one. Already she could sense spring in the air.

An hour later she was poring over several seed catalogues she'd discovered in the office. The diagram of a garden that had been in her mind was now on paper, and she was picking out the varieties of vegetables she wanted to plant. There were so many new hybrids, it was difficult to choose. When the housekeeper returned to the Garrick's ranch, she'd call and ask her advice.

The telephone rang.

"Hello, McCumber ranch," Tess answered.

"Tess? This is Rose."

Tess could tell by the other woman's tone that the news wasn't good. "What's wrong, Rosie?"

"It's your mare, the cream one with the brown patches."

"Yes?" Even as she spoke, Tess felt a premonition of what was to come.

"I accidentally left the gate unlatched. She got out and ran off. I'm terribly sorry, Tess."

"Don't worry. She'll come home as soon as she gets lonely. She's gotten out before."

"My father said she had been waiting for the chance to escape. A wild stallion has been trying to get at the remuda for a month. He thinks she's gone with the rogue."

Tess started laughing. "So she answered his call."

"What? Tess, are you all right?" Rose demanded. "I'm talking about Patches, your prize horse."

"I know. It's okay, really. She'll come to no harm. The Appaloosa has two of the McCumber mares. When Carson recaptures them, I'll get Patches back. Thanks for calling me."

"How's everything going over there? We haven't seen any explosions from the ridge yet."

"You weren't looking at the right time. We've had our ups and downs, you might say."

"Who's winning?" Rose asked.

"I am for the moment, I think." She thought of last night. Carson's defenses had been down then. A few more nicks in his armor and she'd slip right through and into his heart. She hoped. She remembered something else. "Do you know how to make your mother's veal loaf? It was delicious."

Rose laughed. "So you're trying the old adage, 'The way to a man's heart is through his stomach.'"

"Well, I have to start somewhere. Do you have the recipe?"

"Yes. Get a pencil and paper. I'll give it to you."

"I'm ready," Tess said, the sharpened end of the pencil poised over the paper.

At lunch, Carson came in without waiting for the horn blast. Tess saw him sniff appreciatively when he entered the back door.

"The hen house is ready," he said. He removed his muddy boots, then went to the pantry and washed up in the big sink.

"For a bachelor, you're quite neat," she commented when they sat at the table.

Carson smiled. "My mother wasn't above using my granddad's razor strap to prove a point."

"That must have hurt," Tess said sympathetically. "My father was strict, but my mom was a pushover for a sad tale and tears."

Carson laid a large slice of veal loaf on his plate and covered it with gravy. He handed the platter to her and took the bowl of green peas she passed to him. "I've never seen you cry," he said, "not even when..."

"I was sent to the car that time?" she finished when he stopped suddenly. "Or the time you told me to leave you alone? You should have seen me the first week at college."

"Did you cry?" he asked in a strange voice, as if the words were hard to get out.

"Every night." She smiled. "I was the most homesick dogie you ever saw."

The unreadable shadows flickered through his eyes again, and she wondered what he was thinking. Did he feel sorry for her? Or did he think she was a spoiled rich brat who couldn't make it on her own?

A good question. Was she just being stubborn and determined to get her own way with Carson? What was love, anyway? She ate slowly and considered the possible answers.

She remembered how she had felt at college, wanting every semester to speed by so she could go home on the off chance that she would see Carson in town or on the road. The yearning to be with him had never stopped, not during all those years. It had eaten at her insides until her stomach burned and ached.

With a start, she realized her stomach hadn't bothered her at all since her decision to force the issue between them. Other than a momentary twinge when she thought he was hurt, she added. That seemed like a good sign.

She glanced up to see him studying her intently. "The, uh, meat loaf is good," he mumbled, apparently disconcerted to be caught staring at her. He needn't have worried. She could read nothing in the dark depths of his eyes.

"I'm going to be working in the corral this afternoon. I need to fix it up before bringing the calves in for branding." He finished the last of his food, wiped his mouth on the napkin and stood. He gave a brief laugh. "I don't know why I bother. I won't have any more calves in the near future. I won't need to use the open range."

"In case of rustlers?" Tess suggested.

"If I see any, I'll *give* them the scrawny beasts. Save me the vet bills and trouble to raise them."

"Oh, Carson, I nearly forgot," she called when he started out the door. "The Appaloosa has added my mare to his herd. If you decide to go after your two, I want to go and get Patches back."

"So the shoe is on the other foot now," he said.

Tess lifted her eyebrows at him as she carried their plates to the kitchen sink. "Meaning?"

"When it was my mares, your sympathy was for the stallion. Now that it's your property, you want to chase him down. And probably shoot the beast."

"Not at all. That is, I want Patches back. She's not used to the rough life of a range animal. But I wouldn't mind if she became pregnant first. Hmm, in fact, I'd like to take a crack at taming the stallion." Her face brightened. "He'd make a wonderful stud for cow ponies. What a line we'd get with Patches as the dam. Think of it, Carson!" She turned to him, excitement dancing in her eyes.

"Right. I'm thinking there'd be feed and straw and shots to pay for, not to mention the price of a good trainer—"

"Whoa right there, McCumber," she ordered. "You're looking at a darned fine trainer, if I do say so myself. You can ask Dev or Zed or anybody. I'm great with horses."

"For how long?" he asked, a slow, sardonic smile

spreading over his handsome features as if he'd gotten the best of her. "It takes years to establish a reputation and a stud."

"I've got the time."

She didn't let her gaze waver as he challenged her without words. Finally, with a snort of disbelief, he left.

Tess let her breath out on a grateful sigh. She wasn't sure she could have held his gaze much longer. A sense of elation ran through her. Now, at last, she had a plan that could help put the ranch on its feet without her mentioning her money again. If they could capture the stallion. If she could tame it. If the offspring turned out good...

Pipe dreams, ol' girl, she warned her fast-beating heart. But dreams were worth a chance. Weren't they?

Carson explained his plan for capturing the horses right after breakfast the next morning. "We'll run them into the box canyon where the creek starts. I've got a pair of horses staked out along the route so we can switch to fresh mounts."

Tess nodded from the sink where she rinsed the breakfast dishes. She was a little sore from her exertions of the previous day. During the afternoon she had tempted most of the stray hens with corn, thrown a burlap sack over their heads and conveyed them to the hen house. When that tactic hadn't worked with some of the hens, she had chased them down and carried them, squawking and flapping their wings, to the enclosure. "Now lay some eggs and earn your keep," she had admonished, latching the door securely behind her when the last old biddy was inside and sitting on a fresh nest of straw.

Glancing out the kitchen window, she saw the new shingles gleaming on the corner of the hen house visible beyond the stable. The fact that Carson had taken time out of his schedule to do that at her request touched a soft spot inside her. Now he was including her in the roundup of the mares.

"Got that?" he asked.

"Yes. I'll keep them moving from the rear," she said, repeating his instructions.

"Let's go," he said when she dried her hands.

They rode out on two geldings and picked up a fresh trail right away. The sun was out, but another front had moved in, promising another blizzard or sleety rain. The ground had frozen into a hard crust again. The water had stopped running into the creeks and arroyos.

When the stallion spotted the two riders invading his territory, a small secluded valley just beyond the ranch house, he sounded a warning to the three mares. Patches wheeled and threw her head into the air but didn't run. She neighed in excitement as she picked up the riders' scent.

Tess saw the stallion nip at Patches's flanks, then bite to get her to run. The other two followed.

"Naturally your mare is the dominant one," Carson muttered, also watching the action. "Okay, let's head'em up and move'em out." With a wild whoop, he thundered off after the small herd. Tess rode beside him, adding her cry to his.

When Carson wheeled to the left to head them toward the canyon, Tess continued behind the herd, using her rope and shouts to keep the horses running and confused. They headed toward the box canyon that divided the Garrick property from the McCumber ranch, Patches racing in front while the stallion stopped to issue a challenge and fight the newcomers. The snap of Carson's whip sent him on his way again.

When their mounts tired, another set waited along the route. Quickly they threw their saddles on the fresh horses and started off again, driving the others relentlessly toward the west. When they entered the canyon, the driven herd splashed across the small creek that flowed from the cliff enclosing the far end. Tess paused on a hillock and watched the final action.

Carson rode as one with his mount, his entire being intent on the task before him. He and the dark brown gelding were beautiful together. Ah, if only she were an artist!

When he pulled up and fell in behind the racing mares and the stallion, she circled to the right. Together they drove the animals into the temporary stockade.

Carson turned to her, his face alight with their success. "We got the son of a gun!"

Tess rode up beside Carson. "Hurray for our side," she sang out, laughing with him.

Unconsciously, he leaned toward her. As natural as sunshine, she lifted her face for his kiss. Their lips almost met before he realized what was happening and settled back in his saddle.

"We'll both get ropes on him and take him back to the ranch. My mares will follow. Will yours?"

"Patches won't be left behind."

They entered the makeshift paddock and rode past the strand of trees near the wall of granite. Carson's mares were drinking, their sides heaving, their skin twitching with nervous excitement. Patches and the stallion were nowhere to be seen.

"This is the craziest thing I've ever encountered," Carson remarked half an hour later. They'd gone in opposite directions and ridden the entire canyon. The two horses had disappeared as if a genie had scooped them up and made off with them.

"They have to be inside the stockade," Tess said. "I saw them both go in with my own eyes."

"Yeah. Tell me where they are now."

Tess heard the frustration in his voice. He was a man who hated to be thwarted. The last five years must have taken their toll on his nerves, too. She turned her head so he wouldn't see the sympathy in her eyes.

"Well, we got your mares. Let's take them back to the stable." She glanced at her watch. "It'll be time for lunch before we get back."

"You don't look too disappointed about your mare."

Tess gave him a challenging glance over her shoulder as she put a lead rope on one of the mares. "I told you I wanted to start a new line from Patches and the stallion. Let's leave them in here for a couple of days. He might come more willingly then."

She saw a light flare in Carson's eyes before he, too, roped a mare. A sardonic grin touched his mouth before he spoke. "He wouldn't be the first male to let himself get caught due to some female's charms."

"Nor the last," she retorted.

A long second elapsed before Carson laughed harshly. "Some males have more sense."

"And others have less."

The oblique conversation verged on a quarrel. Before it could develop, Tess grinned cockily and turned for the house. "Come on, cowboy. We have a long ride ahead of us before we reach home."

"A long, long ride," she heard him mutter behind her.

Rose called Saturday morning. Tess had just finished gathering eggs from the five setting hens and threatening the other three with the stew pot if they didn't produce.

"Hello, McCumber ranch."

"Tess, this is Rose. How's it going?"

"Fine." Tess told of the chase the day before.

"You didn't get Patches?" Rose sounded stricken with guilt.

"Don't worry. She's penned up with the stallion. I'm hoping they'll mate."

"A wild Appaloosa with your prize horse?"

"Yes. Anything else on your mind?"

"Well, the reason I called...does Carson have room to hire another hand?"

Tess thought of his working all alone. "He sure does."

"Do you think it would be all right if I sent someone over? It's my husband's uncle, Ramon Montagna."

"Has he had any experience on a ranch?"

"Only in picking vegetables," Rose admitted, "but he's willing to learn. He's a good carpenter, too, and could make repairs or build anything. He did new cabinets for me in L.A."

"What's he doing here?"

"He wanted to get his sons away from the city. Drugs and all. You know how it is. He's been doing odd jobs for the past year. He's had a hard time."

"I don't know," Tess began. "Can't Zed take him on?"

"No. He says he has all the hands he can use."

At the discouraged note in her friend's voice, Tess made a decision. "Tell him to come over for an interview with Carson about, um, five this afternoon. He'll have to take the long way around. The ridge road is too muddy."

"Great. Thanks, Tess. I really appreciate this. Uncle Ramon is a wonderful person and a good worker. You'll see. Bye, and thanks." Rose hung up.

Tess replaced the receiver. She'd probably hear it when Carson yelled at her for interfering in his business again, but a friend is a friend is a friend, she reminded herself. Besides, he needed help desperately.

She checked the time. She had hours to think of something to convince him to hire the man.

Carson was furious.

"Who made you my secretary?" he demanded. "Did I tell you to set up appointments for me?"

"I know you're exasperated with me," she said soothingly. "But think a minute—"

"Believe me, I am," he snapped, tossing his boots into the bench and stalking over to glare at her. "I'm thinking of all the things I should have done when you first arrived, before I let you get a toehold in here. Now you think you're the manager."

"Thanks for the promotion," she quipped, not very wisely. She waited for the first flurry of his anger to die down.

He placed his hands on her shoulders and turned her from the pot roast. "Don't drive me too far," he muttered, his gaze going to her mouth.

"It won't hurt to talk to the man."

Carson sighed. "I suppose not. But I don't have any money to hire him."

"You could—"

"I don't want to hear about your money!"

"—borrow back some of the money you've paid off on the note," she went on ruthlessly, "and pay wages out of it. In a couple of years, you'd be better off."

"That's what I thought five years ago." His smile held no trace of humor.

He released her, looking tired beyond his years. He was stretched to the limit of his endurance, she realized. When was the last time he had had a good night's sleep, free of worry and a load of work that would daunt Hercules?

"I know," she said gently.

"Don't pity me, Tess. I can take a lot from you, but that's not on the list. I'll make it without your help."

She nodded. She knew about pride. "I'll tell Rose's uncle we don't need him. Are you ready for supper? You're in a little early tonight."

"I have some work in the office I need to do first." He walked over to the door to the hall. "I guess I can talk to the man when he comes. Send him in the office."

"Okay," she said, managing to hide her surprise. Honestly, men were the most changeable creatures on earth. She poked the roast with a fork. It was done. She turned the burner to low and went into the living room to start a fire.

A car drove up a few minutes later towing a small trailer with wooden side rails and covered with a tarpaulin. The car contained not only a man but a woman and several children. About five, she thought. Oh, dear. She went to the door before the bell rang.

"Mr. Montagna? Come in. I'm Tess Garrick. Carson is in the office. Right this way." She was talking much too fast.

When she entered the office, Carson was at the window. He turned to face her, his eyes opaque. She gave him a beseeching look. *Be kind,* she silently pleaded. *All those children.* A flicker of emotion passed through his eyes, but she didn't know what it was.

"Thank you, Tess," he said, dismissing her. "Carson McCumber," he said to the short, thin man who stood quietly in the center of the room, his hat clutched in front of him with both hands. "Oh, Tess, please invite his family in for a warm drink." He pushed her out and firmly closed the door behind her.

In a few minutes the five young Montagnas, all boys, were seated on the living room floor in front of the fire, sipping hot chocolate. Mrs. Montagna, with dark hair and Spanish eyes, perched on a chair. She and Tess talked about the weather. Each time the group heard a sound from across the hall, all seven pairs of eyes turned that way. There was such hope and despair in the mother's gaze that Tess had to look away.

"So you think you'd like to be a rancher?" she said brightly to the oldest boy, who was maybe fourteen. He nodded shyly. "It's a lot of hard work. You have to get up early."

"Carl gets up very early," one of the younger boys informed her. He was obviously proud of his older brother. "He is smart and very strong. He can lift three of us at once! When Papa hurt his back, Carl did all his work for a week."

So that was the problem. The man had been hurt.

"Ramon is all right now," Mrs. Montagna assured Tess.

The men were closeted in the office for over an hour. When the door opened, Tess let out a breath of relief. The strain of waiting had been terrible. Carson came into the living room.

"Can we put them up tonight, Tess?" he asked. "Tomorrow Ramon and I will fix up the foreman's house."

"Yes," she said, surprised nearly to speechlessness.

"This is too much trouble," Mr. Montagna protested. "My niece—"

"It's no trouble at all." Tess recovered her poise and hastily made plans. "There's a bedroom for the adults. Would you boys mind roughing it on the floor in here?"

A chorus of enthusiasm greeted her. Soon she was giving out orders and bedding to the five. "What is your name?" she asked the middle one, who was the most talkative. He was telling her of an adventure he'd had in the city.

"Richard," he told her.

"Okay, Richard, here's your sheet and blanket. Can you roll up in it like a cowboy would out on the range?"

"Sure."

"After supper, you can show me." She looked around. Everyone had bedding and had claimed a place on the floor. Mr. Montagna had gone to the car to get their luggage. Tess spoke to Mrs. Montagna. "The bathroom's right here, towels in here." She showed her the locations.

"Thank you so much, Miss Garrick," the woman said with grave dignity.

"Call me Tess, if you don't mind. We're not very formal around here."

"And I am Rachel."

"Good. Does your family like pot roast? It's ready—"

"No, no, that is too much trouble. We have sandwiches in the car for our dinner."

"You'll need them tomorrow for lunch. Carson will thank you for eating the roast, else he'll get it all week."

"That's right," Carson drawled, joining them in the hall. "Tess only fixes it to torture me. She knows I love hamburgers."

"Me, too," Richard spoke up, his black eyes alight.

"Well, it's pot roast tonight," Tess informed them. "If you're good, maybe we'll have hamburgers tomorrow night."

"We'll be very good," Richard promised. He glanced at Carson, suddenly not sure of his ground. "Won't we, sir?"

Carson looked at Tess with a cryptic smile. "As good as we possibly can be," he said solemnly.

She couldn't figure him out. What was he up to? "Well, come on into the kitchen, then. Supper's ready."

Soon the five boys and two men were seated at the large table. Tess and Rachel carried dishes from the stove and passed them around. As the other children overcame their shyness, they began to talk and laugh. Carson told them about the Appaloosa outsmarting him and Tess. He told them about the work there was to be done on the ranch.

Tess realized he was instructing Mr. Montagna in the process without the man having to ask questions and appear ignorant in front of his children.

So, she thought, he does have a heart, after all. She

glanced down at the table. He was watching her play hostess to the family. For a second she saw into the shadows and recognized pain. Was he remembering happier times at this table, when he had been younger and his family had been gathered there to share their day as well as food?

There can be other times like that, her eyes promised. If you'd but let them.

He looked away before she could see an answer.

Chapter Five

"The boys had woke up when Tess tiptoed into the kitchen to put on the coffee and fix Carson's breakfast. For once she had gotten up before Carson did.

"Didn't sleep well last night?" she asked him sweetly as they drove along the road, heading for the foreman's house. The day was warm and sunny, as if the blizzard of a week ago had never been. That could mean more flash floods to worry about.

The Montagna family, pulling their trailer of household goods, was in their car behind them, kids hanging out of every window. Carson flicked a wry glance her way before concentrating once more on missing the worst potholes. "I was wondering how I was going to feed seven extra people on a budget that wouldn't feed a family of parakeets."

"Are you kidding? This is a ranch," she reminded him. "We have beef on the hoof all over the place.

Rachel and I'll be putting in a garden at the end of the month, then we'll have fresh vegetables. The hens are laying. I'm thinking of buying a hundred fryers for the freezer—''

''Just one minute.'' He was silent for a moment. ''Look, I agree we need an extra hand, but a family—''

''Did you see their faces this morning, Carson? Look at them. They're laughing and happy and relaxed. They have a home and a job. They have prospects, as Zed would say. Remember?''

He remembered. A man has to have prospects of making a life for his family to feel he's a man, Zed had said more than once during the time Carson had worked at the Garrick ranch. So what did that make him? He could barely afford to keep himself. How was he going to provide for seven others? Not to mention Tess.

''You gave that to them,'' Tess said softly. She knew her feelings were shining in her eyes. She couldn't help it. Carson had done a good thing for the Montagnas, and she was proud of him.

He turned off the main road onto a gravel driveway. The truck bounced in and out of the rain-washed holes. ''I'll grade the road as soon as it dries out a bit more.'' He stopped in front of a modest log house with a split-rail fence around the yard. It was set back from the road in a little grove of pines and sycamores, and just a quarter of a mile from the main house.

''Carson, this is lovely,'' Tess said. ''It looks perfect.''

''My father and I built it one summer from a kit. I

smashed my fingers more than once, but I learned a lot about carpentry.''

So not all the memories were bad. She was glad. ''It doesn't look in need of repair.''

''The roof is deteriorating.'' He pointed out the spots.

Mr. Montagna stopped his car behind them and climbed out. ''This is it?'' he asked. He looked at the roof. ''A simple repair. I can do it in three hours.''

The men removed a roll of shingles from the truck and set to work. Tess and Rachel went inside. Three bedrooms and an attic room provided ample sleeping space. The kitchen and living room were large and comfortable.

Later that afternoon, with their furniture installed and the attic and sheds of the main house searched through for extra pieces, the Montagnas were settled in.

''Well, that didn't take terribly long, did it?'' Tess commented, stretching her tired muscles after she climbed in the pickup beside Carson.

It was dusk. They had put in twelve hours on the log house that day. The evening chores still had to be done, but supper was over. Carson had grilled hamburgers for the entire gang, and they had eaten al fresco off paper plates on the screened back porch.

Tess wrapped her arms around herself as Carson drove off. The night air was cold and she wore only a light jacket. Glancing behind her, she saw firelight through the picture window.

''Carson, look. Ramon has made a fire for them. Doesn't that look cozy?''

He glanced around before pulling onto the country road. A strange expression crossed his face. For a moment, Tess thought she saw pain and longing there, then it was gone and he was the tough rancher once more, showing no emotion.

"No home fires burning for us," she commented when they reached the dark ranch house. She jumped out as soon as he stopped the truck. Inside, she turned on lights and struck a match to the firewood he'd laid that morning. Carson went to the stables. When he didn't return soon, she peered anxiously out the window. He was standing by the corral, his arms resting on the top rail while he stared into the distance.

He looked so alone.

But he didn't have to be, she realized. She was there. Together they could accomplish everything their hearts desired. She was sure of it. She turned from the window and stared wistfully into the flames.

By Thursday, Tess wondered how they had ever gotten along without the Montagnas. On Monday, Carl had appeared when she started the morning chores at the stables. He had watched every move she made. The next morning when she went out, she found all the tasks had been performed flawlessly. When she thanked him, he told her solemnly that he would take care of the horses if she would guide him. On Wednesday, George, the next oldest son, had joined Carl and learned from him.

Tess saw Carson teach Ramon how to saddle up and drive the cattle. On the following Tuesday, Carl and George had joined them. The two youngest boys stayed at home with Rachel. Richard, the middle one, attached himself to Tess.

"Careful of this one," she said on Thursday morning. They were gathering eggs.

"Does she bite?" Richard asked, standing back.

"She pecks." Tess showed him the scab on her hand from a previous encounter. "If she wasn't such a good layer, she'd be in the stew pot before you could say 'this old biddy sat on a tack.'"

He laughed, delighting her with his smile and sparkling eyes and the dimples that flashed in his cheeks. He'd be a heartbreaker someday. Like another she could name, she thought, looking out the hen-house door at the sound of horses galloping into the yard.

She was disappointed when she saw only Carl and George. She'd hoped Carson would come in for lunch, but with the spring roundup, that was a forlorn wish. She'd send sandwiches back with the boys.

"How's it going?" she called.

"Okay," George answered.

"Fine," Carl said at the same time.

They were evidently men of few words. All of the boys, she had noted, tried to imitate Carson's mannerisms from the way they spoke right down to the way they wore their hats and sat on their horses. Their own father had little to say. They'd all make perfect cowboys.

She ducked back into the hen house. Richard had already gathered the rest of the eggs from under the hens. "Very good. Take them to your mother as a present from me and you."

She smiled when he scampered off. Other than her

nephew, she hadn't been around children much, but she found the Montagna boys a delight. She considered having children of her own.

The girls in college had talked about it some, and she'd always assumed that children were in her future, but she'd never tried to visualize them. Now she found herself wondering if they'd have light brown hair and eyes like hers or dark like Carson's. If she had sons with him, would their eyes be filled with mysterious shadows that hid their feelings from the world?

Remembering the curtain material that awaited her at the house, she started across the yard. Carson had opened an account for her and one for Rachel at the dry-goods store. He'd told her to get what she needed and he'd take care of the bills. She hadn't questioned him, but she'd wondered how much money he had.

The low whicker of one of the cow ponies caught her attention. She looked up. A horse galloped toward her. With a glad neigh, Patches dashed up, wheeled and started off again. She stopped and looked at Tess expectantly.

"Patches, there you are! What are you up to?" Tess called after the animal. She or one of the boys had checked the box canyon several times but had seen nothing of the stallion or the mare. Obviously they'd jumped the temporary fence.

The mare pranced nervously, came to Tess, nudged her shoulder and bounded off again.

"You want me to go with you?" Tess questioned. "Come here, then. Steady now," she crooned when she got close enough to touch the mare. Grabbing a handful of mane, she swung herself onto the horse's back. It had been a while since she'd ridden bareback, but she didn't have her saddle and the boys needed theirs.

Once Tess was seated, the mare took off in a gallop, eager to be gone. She was heading for the ridge. Carson and Ramon were working over that way.

The ride was a long one. Tess was tired, her backside aching, by the time the mare dropped down the rocky incline to an arroyo that split the canyon along one side. The horse stopped on the ledge and whickered softly.

Tess dismounted and peered over the edge.

The stallion was there, lying on his side in a tangle of barbed wire. He tried to rise, but the struggle was useless. He was bound tightly. Tess knew she needed help.

"Patches, here. Come, girl, we have to get help."

The mare didn't want to leave, but Tess was firm. They needed Carson. It was an hour before they found him, working a chaparral thicket just below the ridge.

"Carson," Tess yelled, seeing him ride into another dense stand of brush.

He reappeared immediately. Giving his horse the spur, he raced toward her. "What is it?" he demanded, his eyes running over her as if to make sure she had no injury.

"The stallion is trapped in a tangle of barbed wire. You've got to come. Do you have your wire cutters?"

"Yes," he said impatiently. "What are you doing on that horse? Where's your saddle?"

She shook her head at the questions. "Patches

came to me and wanted me to go with her, a trick she learned when she wanted me to pick an apple for her—''

''All right, spare the history. Where's the stallion?''

''This way.''

In her eagerness to be off, the mare nearly unseated Tess. Behind her, Carson swore, then swooped down on her. He lifted Tess off of Patches with an arm around her waist and sat her in front of him on his horse.

''There. Maybe you won't break your fool neck now,'' he muttered, kicking the gelding into a canter.

She made an indignant protest, then fell silent as they rode across the dirt. Carson's heart beat steadily against her back while her own thundered against her ribs like a stampeding herd. She wondered if he could discern what he did to her just by being this close.

''Sit still,'' he ordered.

His harsh tone caused her to stiffen her spine. For fifty yards she rode with the grace of a stick. He heaved an exasperated sigh. ''Relax. You're driving me right up the wall.''

''What do you think you're doing to me?'' she snapped. ''You should have left me on Patches instead of acting like a movie hero.''

''You nearly fell off. I didn't want to have to pay your doctor bills when you broke your neck.''

''Then quit complaining.''

An arm encircled her waist and his hand clasped her in a firm grip. ''Who's complaining?'' he murmured in her ear.

She swiveled her head around to stare at him. He met her gaze with a puckish smile on his lips and simmering desire in his eyes. ''Just shut up and ride,'' he advised.

''I'll try.'' She forced herself to relax against him. Soon they were riding as one on the gelding. He urged the horse to a faster pace.

As soon as they crossed the ridge, a whicker of welcome greeted them. Patches ran toward Tess, then wheeled and dashed a short ways across the rocky outcropping. The mare paused and looked back at the slower moving humans.

''The Appaloosa is in the arroyo,'' Tess explained.

''He's lucky the water isn't more than a dribble now. It was almost full a few days ago.'' Carson glanced at the drifts of snow under the trees. ''And will be again.''

''I know.'' Apprehension formed a knot in her throat. What if they were unable to get the stallion out? They reached the narrow gully. ''Let me down.''

He leaned backward and gave her room to swing her leg over the saddlehorn, then he lowered her to the ground with a hand around her wrist.

Tess peered over the edge. ''He's tried to get free again, I think. His position has changed a bit.'' She scrambled down the loose gravel and dirt. A rope swung over her head and clamped her arms to her sides, stopping her mad dash to the bottom. ''Let me go,'' she cried.

''Not until I see what shape the stallion is in.'' Carson was just as furious as she. ''That's a wild animal. Do you want your brains kicked out?''

Carson dismounted and loosened the tension on the rope. Tess threw it over her head. "He's tangled in barbed wire. He couldn't hurt a fly."

"Let's proceed with caution." Carson went down the steep bank first, keeping an eye on the Appaloosa. "We'll circle around him and come in from the front so he can see what we're doing."

The horse tried to toss its head and bare its teeth at them, but it was too weak for even that effort. It closed its eyes and lay still.

"Carson, he's really hurt." Tess couldn't keep the quiver out of her voice. Only last week the stallion had been wild and free. Now he was caught in a man-made trap as cruel as a leg shackle. The barbs had dug into his flesh as he'd tried to free himself, leaving deep gashes. He'd have scars for life. "How long do you think he's been like this?"

"At least a couple of days. He's exhausted. Dammit, be careful," Carson barked when she bent over the injured animal. "I'll go get my gun."

"Gun? What for?" She saw the answer in his eyes. "No! You're not going to shoot him."

"He's near death already. It would be the kindest thing to do." Carson gave an impatient jerk on his hat. "And it'll stop him from running off with any more mares."

"I won't let you shoot him, not without giving him a chance. He's cold," she said, running a hand over his nose and ears. "He'll die of exposure if he spends another night like this. We've got to get him to the stable and warm him up."

Her eyes were defiant when she faced Carson. They

waged a silent battle before he clenched his jaw and gave in. ''First we have to cut him free.'' He pulled the wire cutters from his back pocket. ''I'd better tie his legs.''

''No, don't,'' Tess protested. ''He hasn't the strength to kick. He can hardly lift his head.''

Carson frowned, but he didn't insist. While Tess held the stallion's head, he cut the wire into pieces and moved it a safe distance away. ''We'll have to stand him up to get the ones under him.'' He went to get his rope.

Tears came to Tess's eyes when the stallion whickered in pain as they worked with him. They had to push the rope under him and make a sling. After tying the end to the saddle, Carson backed the gelding until the rope pulled tight, then slowly they lifted the stallion to his feet. Tess pulled the rest of the wire away from his body.

''Okay, that's it,'' Carson said when they were finished. ''We've done all we can. He'll have to make it on his own.''

''Can we pull him out?'' she called up. ''We can't just leave him here. He'll be cougar bait. Please,'' she added.

''If you can get the mare to help, we could.'' Carson said in a resigned tone. Tess gave him her most grateful smile.

Following Carson's instructions, Tess looped some of the rope around the mare's neck. Working as a team of four and using a tree for a pulley, they managed to haul the stallion up the bank. He moved his feet feebly, trying to break free and run. Once on top, his legs collapsed under him. They gently lowered him to the ground.

"We need a fire," Tess decided. "Gather some wood."

"Yes, ma'am."

She paid no attention to Carson's cynical reply, but promptly began rubbing the stallion's neck and talking softly to him. Patches whinnied and pranced nervously before nudging Tess. Tess stroked the velvety nose and soothed her mare before turning her attention back to the stallion. "He's in a bad way, old girl," she murmured. "But we'll save him."

Carson didn't say anything, but after making a fire ring with stones, he started a blaze near them. "I'm going back to the house for the medicine kit. I'll bring some food. This is going to be a long siege," he predicted.

Surprised, Tess watched him ride off. When he returned in the pickup, pulling the horse trailer, she was more perplexed. He made no move to load the horses. After covering the stallion with a blanket, he served food. After making Tess eat a sandwich and drink a thermos of lemonade, he gave the horse a shot of antibiotics, then mixed a soupy hot mash and forced some down the stallion's throat. Then he pitched a tent and unrolled a sleeping bag and pad in it.

Patches, obviously sure that everything was going to be all right now, ate her bag of oats with relish.

"Are we spending the night?" Tess asked, eyeing the tent. A lightning bolt of sensation rushed along her spine. She was suddenly nervous.

"Unless you think you can get the stallion on his

feet and keep him there until we make the trip back to the stable.''

''No, he can't stand that long.''

''He'll need to be fed every couple of hours and given water more often. He's dehydrated.''

She nodded. Although the stallion bared his teeth at her every once in a while, that was the extent of his defiance. She dripped water into his mouth from her bandanna. By midnight, he was accepting food from her more easily.

''Okay,'' Carson said when she finished another feeding. ''You go to bed. I'll take over for the rest of the night.''

Tess shook her head. ''You sleep. I'm not tired.''

He gave a little snort. ''That's why your hand is trembling. I suppose, because you're so full of energy. Hit the sack, Tess. That's an order from the boss.''

She looked up with a laugh. ''I've been demoted again. It's hard to know what my position is with you.''

''One day I'll tell you,'' he said, the slashes appearing at each side of his mouth as he smiled. He tilted his head toward the tent. ''Are you going, or do I have to carry you?''

The answer she wanted to give was on the tip of her tongue, but she bit it back. Undefined feelings rioted through her, leaving her confused and vulnerable. While he smiled and joked with her, her whole world went into a tailspin.

''I'll go.'' She stood and stretched, letting her coat fall off her shoulders as she did. The next thing she knew, she was caught up against a hard male body. Her heart thudded painfully.

"Don't play with me, Tess," Carson said in a husky voice. "We're alone out here, playing nursemaid to a damned nuisance of a wild horse, and my temper is running thin."

"So what else is new?" she asked, rubbing her palms up and down his arms. Keep it light, she admonished. But she wanted so much more than lightness, things such as touching and stroking, things such as words. She needed words of love and endearment.

The tension escalated between them as he stared at her mouth, then let his gaze wander along her throat. "That ride up here nearly drove me crazy," he murmured. "Feeling you against me, knowing how soft and warm you can be, seeing how gentle you are. Don't tempt me beyond control, Tess."

She sensed that he was near a turning point. Should she force the issue? He would make love to her if she encouraged him only a bit. Then what? Wait, a wiser part of her counseled.

"I'll try not to," she whispered. "But I have limits, too."

"I know," he said.

He released her and stepped back. His eyes were suddenly bleak, the fires of a moment ago doused by thoughts she couldn't follow. She walked toward the tent, then glanced back and watched as Carson added more wood to the fire and checked the stallion to see if the animal was warm.

They were alike, she thought, the man and the

beast. Both of them wild creatures who couldn't be forced, not without breaking their spirits. She'd never do that. Each of them must give his trust to her of his own accord. She'd wait.

The stallion was stronger the next day. He made several lunging attempts to get to his feet as his strength returned. Carson finally tied the animal's legs with a hobble.

Carson stayed close, which was a pleasure and a pain for Tess. She loved working with him, but the situation only reminded her of what they could have if he weren't so stubborn. Or if he loved her. The thought that he might not was chilling.

"Here, put this around you," he said, seeing her rub her arms. He dropped her jacket around her shoulders. The night had been cold, but the day was warm. The little rivulets of water were running again, but slowly this time. There'd be no flash floods.

"Thanks." She smiled over her shoulder at him.

"You shouldn't do that," he said.

"What?"

"Smile like that. It gives a man ideas." He walked away. "Believe me, I get enough of those on my own."

For the rest of the day he stayed carefully away from her, but once in a while she could feel his eyes on her. Like the land in springtime, she felt renewed and buoyant with hope. Things were taking a turn for the better.

The last thing she saw before she closed the tent flap and went to sleep that night was Carson rubbing the stallion's ears, the fire burning brightly behind them. The next morning, when she got up, the first thing she saw was the stallion on its feet.

"Easy, easy," Tess said.

The Appaloosa kicked at her, feebly but with determination.

"You overgrown hayburner," she scolded. "Stop acting so tough and behave yourself. It's not too late to call the glue factory."

Richard snickered from behind a wheelbarrow. Carson, with a rope harness on the stallion, was trying to back it out of the trailer and into the paddock. The horse wasn't cooperating. Now that he'd had food and water for forty-eight hours, he was feeling his roguish self.

"Stand back," Carson called impatiently to Tess, who hovered at the end of the ramp as if to rush to the rescue if the stallion seemed about to fall flat. "Get on the fence."

When she was safely out of the way, Carson slapped the stallion on the neck and yelled in his face. The horse bounded backward in surprise. Carson let the rope slip free and ran down the ramp, shooing the stallion farther into the paddock. He pulled the gate closed and fastened it.

Tess, perched on the top rail, laughed as the stallion looked around as if just realizing he'd been tricked. "Gotcha," she said with a gleam of triumph in her eyes.

Carson leaned on the rail beside her. "So what are you going to do with him?"

"Tame him."

"He's been wild too long," Carson advised.

"I'll have him eating out of my hand in a month."

"He's already done that," Carson pointed out.

"I mean *willingly*, not because he's injured and helpless."

She met Carson's keen gaze. A level of understanding passed between them, and each recognized the strength and will of the other to succeed in the struggle between them.

"You could end up breaking your heart if you think you can make another Patches out of this maverick."

The warning in his voice should have been discouraging, but this morning she felt ready to tackle the world.

"I'm not stupid. He'll never be docile—not that Patches is, either—but he'll learn to trust me. Maybe."

"So even the great Tess Garrick can contemplate defeat."

She didn't respond to the barb. Instead she asked, "Did you ever hear of the thief who promised the emperor he would teach his horse to sing in a year if the ruler would stay his execution that long and pardon him if he succeeded?"

Carson gave her a flinty smile. "No."

"When one of the other condemned thieves said it was impossible to teach a horse to sing, the first one replied: Perhaps, but in a year the emperor may die, or the horse may die, or I may die. Or the horse may learn to sing."

Richard rushed up to them. "Can I ride him? Can I?"

Carson gave him a ferocious scowl. "You stay away from this animal. He's wild and frightened of people. He'll kick you clean over the fence if you try to touch him. Understand?"

"Yes. He is dangerous, that one."

"You got it." Carson climbed in the truck and drove off toward the storage barn.

Richard looked at Tess. "He doesn't like the horse?"

She shook her head. "He doesn't like the idea of my trying to tame it. He thinks I'll get hurt."

The boy's eyes opened wide. "The horse will kick you."

"Maybe. Or maybe the horse will learn to sing."

Chapter Six

"There! That's the last one," Tess declared, setting the steam iron on its heel and wiping the perspiration from her face.

Rose brought over a curtain rod and began sliding the material on it. Rachel helped her. Together they carried the curtain to the window and slipped the rod into the holders.

"Lovely, really lovely," Rose said, standing back to admire their work. The material was a soft nubby weave of blue and yellow yarns among the beige ones. An occasional pink yarn added a dash of warmth. The curtains hung in soft pleats and toned the sunlight down to a hazy glow.

"I couldn't have done it without Rachel," Tess explained. "She's the one who showed me what mitering meant and all the rest of the jargon the sewing book seemed to think I should know."

"You did a super job. The pleats hang perfectly. Did Carson grumble about putting up the hardware? My husband always did."

"I didn't ask," Tess confessed. "I did it myself."

Carson had already done more than she had expected. He'd had the vet out to look the stallion over and give it the necessary immunization shots. That had been a job requiring all the males on the place to help. Without her asking, he'd plowed a garden plot big enough that she and Rachel could share.

"You did an excellent job," Rachel complimented.

"It was a simple matter of following directions," Tess said with a dismissive toss of her head.

At that moment Richard burst through the door, the wind rushed in behind him and half the curtains fell down.

The three women burst out laughing.

"So much for my mechanical skills," Tess said, checking her handiwork while Rose and Rachel bent to pick up the curtains. "This time, let's make sure we get them on the right groove."

"Richard, you must knock before you enter, then open the door quietly, not as if you were announcing the end of the world," Rachel scolded. "Let me hear your apology."

He grinned sheepishly, apologized, then remembered to grab the hat off his head before that sin was added to the list. "I wanted to know…I came to ask if I could ride Patches. The boss said I had to ask you first 'cause she's your horse. I'd be careful."

"Is Carson going to stay with you?"

He nodded. "He's going to let me ride with him

to check some fences. If it's all right with you and my mom.''

Tess and Rachel exchanged a glance. Tess nodded. The older woman said, ''It's fine with me, but you do everything you're told.''

''I will.'' He looked at Tess for final approval.

''It's okay with me. Here, take these gingerbread cookies with you. You and Carson might need a snack before supper.'' She put several in a sack and handed them over.

''Oh, boy, gingerbread!'' He was out the door in a flurry of energy, but this time the curtains stayed put.

Rose applauded, and the women adjourned to the living room to plan the garden over coffee and cookies.

''Look what I got,'' Richard said as he rushed up to Carson and came to a breathless halt.

Carson looked up from the small saddle he was polishing and grinned at his helper. ''What is it?''

''Gingerbread cookies. Tess gave 'em to us. Want one? She said we could eat 'em all before supper.''

''Did she now?''

''Yeah, *really*.''

Carson laughed as the boy opened the bag and pulled two huge cookies out. Together they bit into the treat. Carson savored the taste of molasses and spices on his tongue before his thoughts returned to his primary problem of the past three weeks—namely, Tess. What was he going to do about her?

That first week, he'd thought she'd pack up and leave at any moment, but she'd pitched right in and taken over the house and stable without a complaint. He'd thought it would be only a matter of time before she grew bored and fed up with working from morning to night, but still she was there.

The second week, the Montagnas were installed in the log house. He hadn't been able to ignore the plea in her eyes and so he had ended up hiring not just a cowhand, but an inexperienced one at that...and his whole family, to boot.

This week she was decorating the house. She and Rachel had spent every spare moment in the sewing room, making curtains for the kitchen. Next she planned to paint the walls and refinish the cabinets, all this at a fraction of the cost he had expected. Sometimes he found himself just watching her, amazed.

"Come on, cowboy," he said. "Let's see if this saddle fits."

"Where'd you get it?" Richard asked, running his hand over the tooled leather.

"My dad gave it to me when I was about your age. I thought it was the finest saddle in the world."

"It is!"

Richard scampered alongside him to the corral. There, Carson saddled Patches for Richard and a gelding for himself. "Here you go." He lifted the boy onto the saddle. "Wait here for me. Don't move, okay?"

"Okay." Richard sat very still, the reins clutched in his hands, his eyes shining.

Carson felt a hard knot rise to his throat. He remembered other gifts from his father, not extravagant but generously given. There had been good times, he remembered, before his mother died and the drinking had gotten bad. She'd been the center of their lives. When she'd gone, his dad had lost his moorings.

Carson realized he'd been too harsh on his father, blaming him for the condition of the ranch and the emptiness of their lives. Now he could see that other forces had also played a hand.

He entered the kitchen and stopped at the sound of feminine laughter. His gaze made a slow traverse of the room. It looked different. Softer, somehow. He spotted the curtains.

Tess. She'd brought softness to his life. A rancher couldn't afford to be soft, he chided himself. She'd brought laughter and companionship to his days. He'd miss those...when she left.

She'd also brought sleepless nights and the reminder that he was a man with all the natural urges of a man toward a woman. She'd caused his insides to curl with longing and his emotions to go haywire. Maybe things would settle down when she left. Peace and quiet, those were exactly what he wanted.

He looked once more at the room. Thirty bucks worth of material and a few afternoons of labor. Who'd have thought it would make such a difference? He'd see about getting a new sink and flooring. Not because of her, but for the house. It was a wise investment.

Quickly he wrote a note telling the women where he and Richard would be working and when they'd return, then ducked out the back door after stealing four more cookies from the jar. Working men needed nourishment.

Tess stood at the corral late that afternoon, holding out an apple just as she'd done every day since they'd brought the stallion home. The horse eyed her suspiciously. She said nothing, made no move. He edged closer, his desire for the apple plainly at war with his caution of humans.

You're going to have to come to me to get it, she silently told him.

He stamped the ground, then walked forward, his ears twitching. Just when he was three feet from her outstretched hand, Richard came running around the corner of the stable. He stopped when he saw Tess and the horse, but it was too late. The stallion wheeled and raced to the far side of the enclosure.

"I didn't know you were here," Richard apologized. "He was almost close to you, too."

"Almost," Tess agreed. She pushed Richard's hair out of his eyes with an affectionate smile. "It doesn't matter. He wouldn't have come closer today."

"He wouldn't? How can you tell?"

"Woman's intuition."

"Oh." He looked glum.

"Actually, everybody has intuition," she amended.

He looked up, pleased. "I'm going to raise horses when I get grown. I'm going to have a big ranch, just like this one."

"Good. May I come see your horses?"

"Sure!"

"When you get through with all this future socializing, could I get a hand with the current stock?'' a sardonic voice inquired.

''Sure,'' Richard cried again, running toward his hero.

''How about you?'' Carson looked at Tess.

Her heart did two somersaults and a back flip before settling down in its proper place. ''Depends on what you want done.''

''Patches is in...'' He stopped and glanced at the boy. ''Your mare needs to be moved. I thought we'd put her next to this one.'' He indicated the stallion. ''Unless you've changed your mind.''

Tess still wanted to breed the mare to the stallion. ''No, I haven't,'' she stated firmly.

''You're damned determined,'' Carson muttered.

''That's right.''

He shrugged. ''Well, come on, then. Let's have her meet her boyfriend.''

Richard laughed and ran before them to the paddock on the other side of the stable. ''Are they going to get married?'' he called over his shoulder before disappearing around the corner.

''I don't know,'' Carson drawled for Tess's hearing only. ''They might just have a mad, passionate affair.''

''It's marriage or nothing,'' Tess avowed.

''Nothing?''

He was suddenly close to her and there was no room to walk. She turned toward him, backing into the stable wall. He placed his hands on the rough planks, one on each side of her, and leaned slightly toward her.

"Nothing?" he said again.

"Nothing," she whispered, her throat as tight as an unopened cotton boll. His eyes bored into hers.

"When are you leaving?"

The words held no meaning for her. She stared up at him, wanting the sweet heat of his lips on hers. It had been so long.

"I said, when are you leaving? Isn't Garrick and his family due home soon?"

"Not for two more weeks. They rented the condo for six weeks, and they've only been gone four." Tess laid a hand in the middle of his chest to hold him away. She'd thought he wanted to kiss her. He only wanted to get rid of her. With a defiant tilt to her chin, she demanded, "What have I done to displease you now?"

"Nothing. I just wondered, that's all. I'll miss your cooking." He shoved himself off the wall and walked on, leaving her staring after him.

Her cooking! He'd miss her cooking! After all she'd done for him, trying to make a home, to lighten his load, to bring a little fun and laughter in his life—and he'd miss her cooking!

Turning, she slung the apple as far as she could throw. It sailed over the fence and hit the unsuspecting stallion on the rump. The stallion jumped and whirled to face the attacker. He looked confused at seeing nothing but an apple on the ground.

"Serves you right," she muttered, and stalked off to help Richard bring Patches around.

Carson sat at the desk, looking disgustedly at the stack of bills he needed to pay. From the kitchen, as

Tess was drying the dishes and putting them away, he could hear the music of a soft rock station and her clear, sweet voice singing about some love that had gone wrong. In the corral, the stallion pranced and whickered in low tones to his lady love, Patches. Tomorrow Carson would let the two into the same pen. They were ready.

So was he.

He wanted Tess with a constant ache. It was like having a permanent case of the flu. That afternoon he'd come close to pressing her against the stable and kissing the daylights out of her. Instead he'd made himself ask her when she was leaving. That had hurt her.

Better to hurt her now— his conscience began.

Yeah, yeah, yeah, another part of him cut it off.

Gritting his teeth, he got down to work. The courtship in the corral didn't help soothe his libido one little bit.

At eleven, he was only half done, but his eyes wouldn't stay open longer. He pressed a hand over them and rubbed vigorously. No use. Well, he'd rest them just a minute, then finish the bills and be done with it for another month. At least he didn't have to figure any quarterly taxes. He hadn't made any money.

Actually, things weren't going as bad as he'd thought they would when he'd counted his losses during the blizzard. He'd been saving for a new truck, but he could overhaul the old one and make it last one more season. The money to pay Ramon and the boys a half-decent wage for their work came from that account. Next year, with their help, he should do a lot better. Maybe things were taking an upward turn this year.

Since Tess came.

Oh, shut up about her.

A hand on his shoulder startled him into full wakefulness.

"Are you all right?" Tess asked. "It's getting awfully late."

"I'm fine," he muttered, trying not to look at her. She wore a fuzzy pink robe and slippers. The high neckline of an old-fashioned nightgown cupped her throat. He wanted to kiss her right on that spot...just where the ribbon lay over the pulse.

"Carson, I do have a business degree. Would you like for me to post your accounts? Dev lets me keep his books."

He couldn't take the temptation another minute. He was going to reach for her...take that robe off...carry her to the living room sofa...build a fire...remove her gown...make love to her.

"Yeah," he said thickly. "That'd be a help. Go back to bed. I'll be there, uh, going to my room in a minute."

"Do you want to go to church tomorrow? It's Easter Sunday."

"Yes. Right. That'll be fine."

"Are you sure you're all right?"

"Yes," he said through gritted teeth. He rose painfully. His body was stiff. All over. "I'll see you in the morning."

"All right. Good night."

He waited until she left the room, then followed, turning off the lights as he went. He ignored her door and went to his room at the end of the corridor. The day had been one of revelation. He'd realized some things about his father that as a boy he hadn't been able to comprehend.

It had also shown him how susceptible he was to a few simple things like new curtains and homemade cookies. The next thing he knew, he'd be eating out of her hand like that dumb horse probably would end up doing.

The Garricks had a reputaton for getting what they wanted. The question was: why did she want him?

Tess was surprised when Carson drove the truck up to the back stoop to pick her up. The ten-year-old vehicle had been washed and waxed to shining perfection.

"A carriage from a pumpkin," she remarked, climbing in after Carson leaned over and opened the door. "Very nice."

"The boys did it this morning."

"They did a good job. The're good workers, aren't they?"

He gave her an oblique glance that sent her pulses racing. "Yes, they are." He shifted into second, then third. "So are you."

"Why, thank you, sir," she exclaimed softly, and lowered her eyes, then peeked at him from under her darkened lashes.

"You look very pretty today, Miss Garrick. Here."

He handed her a spray of silk roses. "My mother used to wear these."

"Thanks again," she said huskily, her throat closing. She pinned the flowers to the red wool jacket she wore over a navy dress. She eyed his suit, a gun-metal gray that fit his lean form perfectly. He wore dress boots and a soft gray Snowy River hat, which had a lower crown and cockier look than the sedate Stetson. "Where'd you get the hat?"

"My father bought it for me when he went to the rodeo up in Calgary one year." He smiled. "Dad forgot birthdays, but he always brought me a present when he went out of town."

"Umm," she said. There was a different element in his tone when he mentioned his father, as if he thought more kindly of him. Was Carson mellowing toward the man?

She sighed. They'd been together for three weeks, living in the same house, eating together, working together, but she felt no closer to him. There had been moments, brief flares of passion as lasting as Fourth of July fireworks. That wasn't enough.

"Tired?" he asked.

Startled, she pulled herself out of the doldrums. "Heavens, no. Between Rachel and the boys, I hardly have to do anything. The kids've taken over the stable chores, and she and I do the garden together. We have it planned and marked off with string."

For the rest of the trip to the small community church, they talked of the ranch. He told her the count on the spring calves would be better than he'd originally thought "once we finally get all the cattle driven out of the chaparral and counted."

"Great."

They arrived at church. Carson came around and lifted her down, his hands strong and capable at her waist. A shimmer of sensation traversed her body. They went inside to find the Montagnas already there, and squeezed in beside them, taking up an entire bench near the back. Since it was time for the service, Tess didn't get a chance to talk to her old high school chums. She wasn't sure she wanted to. The partnership with Carson was a bit farfetched.

After the sermon, the pastor stood at the door and wished them Godspeed on their return home. "We haven't seen you in a while, Carson," he gently reprimanded. "Not since the nativity pageant."

"Yes, sir. You ought to mention to those people who come every Sunday that they should stay home on Christmas and Easter so it wouldn't be so crowded for the rest of us."

Tess clamped her lips together to keep from laughing. She needn't have bothered. The pastor guffawed. She managed to restrain herself to a snicker or two.

Carson looked angelically innocent and surprised by their laughter. Except for the devilish merriment in his eyes.

"I never thought of it that way," the minister admitted. He winked at Tess. "See if you can't get him in more often."

"I can't do a thing with him," she complained.

Carson took her elbow and guided her down the steps. "You can do anything with me, that's the trouble,'' he corrected in a low voice so no one else could hear.

Tess wanted to pursue that train of thought, but they were interrupted by several friends. The fact that she and Carson had arrived together hadn't gone unnoticed.

''Well, do we have some news here?'' Betty Sue Moreley asked, giving Carson a coy glance. ''I understand Tess has moved to your place. Is this a trial period?''

How had she learned that? News could travel incredibly fast along the country grapevine.

''Tess is my partner,'' Carson said easily.

Betty Sue gave Tess a jealous glance. With a start, Tess realized she felt something of the same emotion. She didn't like the way the other single women played up to Carson, smiling and touching him. Jealousy was the curse of the insecure. If Carson had loved her...

''Ready to go?'' he asked, pulling her hand through the crook of his arm.

Tess felt his protection envelop her like a cloak. ''Yes.''

They left the crowd. Instead of turning toward the ranch, Carson drove them to town. ''I thought you might like a day off,'' he said. ''I made reservations for lunch.''

''Why that was thoughtful of you.'' Her day was shining again. How little it took. A pat on the head and she was delirious.

''You're quiet,'' he commented as he again lifted

her from the high truck. They walked into the restaurant. "You used to talk more."

"So did you," she reminded him.

Their eyes met over the linen-covered table after they were seated by the hostess. Both remembered other times when they had shared their dreams of the future. His had been definite. Hers had not. She hadn't been sure if she wanted to run her own shop or continue to work on the ranch training the cow ponies. Never had she doubted that their futures couldn't be combined.

"We were young then."

"Yes," she agreed, feeling terribly sad all at once.

"Don't," he murmured, watching the tears fill her eyes.

She blinked them away. "I won't embarrass you."

A fierceness replaced his look of concern. "Nothing you do could ever embarrass me."

Her smile was shaky. "Not even when it got you bawled out and fired?"

"Not even then."

Their brief discussion helped resolve a bundle of guilt she'd carried for years. She'd never meant to bring pain to Carson or cause him shame. She'd loved him with the blind passion and self-interest of youth, knowing only what she wanted. It was not until later, during all those lonely nights, that she had realized how difficult she must have made Carson's life.

"Well, look who's here—the elusive twosome," a familiar and unwelcome voice interrupted.

Tess had considered Betty Sue a brat even when she had dated her brother, Tess reflected before smiling up at the other young woman and one of her friends.

"Is this a business luncheon or may we join you?" Betty Sue asked. She flirted prettily with Carson.

"Sure," he said.

The two young women took the empty chairs, Betty Sue choosing the one next to Carson, of course. As far as Tess was concerned, the meal went downhill thereafter. Betty Sue carried on a flagrant flirtation, and Carson gallantly responded with a hint of indulgent humor in his replies.

By the time the meal was over, Tess was furious.

They were silent on the ride home. When Carson stopped at the granite slab by the back door, he leaned across her to let her out. "You're still awfully quiet," he remarked. He was very close.

"Maybe I've learned to keep my thoughts to myself," she told him.

"Yes, I believe you have. I liked the old Tess, though." He settled back on his side of the truck and she climbed out, confused at his gentleness.

She went to her room and changed to clean work clothes. She heard Carson enter the house and leave before she came out. When she went to the kitchen, she saw him at the corral, opening the gate between Patches and the stallion.

The mare acted skittish. She retreated to the far side of her paddock. Carson disappeared into the stable. The stallion walked boldly through the opening. Instead of charging the mare as Tess had feared, he approached tentatively. When he was close enough, he rubbed his cheek against her flank.

Tess went outside and stood on the stoop, watching. Carson appeared and joined her. Together they watched the ritual.

''He's being gentle,'' Tess said with a catch in her throat. ''Patches is...she hasn't...''

''This is her first breeding?'' Carson supplied.

''Yes. She's nervous.''

Carson laughed softly, bringing her gaze to him. ''Don't worry. It'll all happen naturally.''

''Sometimes stallions bite.''

''He won't hurt her.''

For some reason, Tess believed him. ''I have work to do.'' She escaped into the house, feeling foolish for standing there like an anxious mother. However, she kept an eye on the two horses throughout the afternoon and evening. The stallion continued to woo Patches, who seemed unsure of her role in the proceedings. Tess laughed once when the mare bared her teeth and the stallion rapidly backed off.

''She's playing hard to get,'' Carson remarked, entering the room and standing behind Tess at the kitchen window.

''Something I never did,'' she said recklessly.

''No,'' he agreed. ''You were always one to go after what you wanted.'' He chuckled at her wry grimace.

He took off his boots and went into the pantry to wash up at the big sink while she put supper on the table. She felt his absence as a disappearance of warmth along her back.

After eating, he went to the office and she read on

the sofa by the fire. He came into the living room a few minutes later.

"You did all the paperwork," he said in disbelieving tones. "And filed everything."

"It was easy. Your system is very orderly."

"I'm impressed. Thanks. That saved me hours of work."

A warm glow permeated her skin. "I had the time."

He took a seat and picked up a ranching magazine. She tried to return to her reading, but his lean, virile presence disturbed her. She felt as nervy as Patches, positive that something vital was in the air, but not sure what.

Once, when she glanced up, she found his eyes on her, dark and brooding. He looked back at his article. An hour passed. The night sky brightened as a half-moon came up over the mountains. The tension became a third entity in the room.

Tess went to the kitchen and got a drink. Standing by the sink with the light off, she watched the two horses circle each other, then stand quietly, just touching. Patches hadn't accepted him yet, but she seemed less nervous. Tess smiled in approval of the stallion's patient seduction.

She was aware of Carson entering silently and standing behind her again. His body heat embraced her. An ache started in some undefined place inside her.

"Sure you want this?" he asked. "Patches is a prize horse with a pedigree. He's a mongrel."

Tess stirred impatiently. "She's a cow pony. He's

a master of the range. I hope to pair her intelligence with his cunning, her conformation with his strength, her agility with his quickness. I want to introduce his tough sense of survival to the line we develop. Blooded stock tends to lose that."

They remained there in the dark, not speaking. The objects in the ranch yard became highlighted in silver as the moon rose. In the paddock, looking no more substantial than the shadows around them, the Appaloosa consummated his courting of the mare.

Carson laid his arm around Tess as a shiver went through her. They returned to the fire-lit living room. He turned the lamp off, leaving them enclosed in a rosy glow.

"I want to touch you like that," he said. He reached for her, his hands clasping her shoulders, his thumbs making little circles of fire on her skin through her sweater.

The suppressed passion flared between them, a conflagration of longing that had been held in check for days…years. She was no longer seventeen, eager to grab all that life offered; he was no longer twenty-three, impatient for success. They faced each other as a man and a woman who had been tested by life, whose needs were no less demanding but were tempered by experience.

She smiled slightly. "I want it, too."

With a muffled imprecation, he pulled her close. She felt a single tremor race over his hard body as they touched. With gentle hands, she rubbed his back, soothing the doubts that assailed him. He wasn't a man to make love to a woman with no thought of tomorrow, and he wasn't sure of their future.

"I want to touch you, smell you, taste you, feel you." He gave a low groan of impatience as he held her closer.

The sofa was at the back of her knees, and she felt the downward movement of their bodies until they reclined in one corner. His arms locked them tightly together.

It was heaven, just being like that with him. She knew it wouldn't be enough for either of them, but for now, for this one moment, she took comfort from lying there with him.

"I used to dream of this, of lying snuggled up to you, a warm fire in the grate, safe from the wind and storms outside," she whispered dreamily.

"What of the storms inside?" he asked. His lips touched her face, a warm exploration along her cheek.

"I wasn't afraid of those."

"Are you now?"

"No."

He took her hand, guided it to his chest. "Can you feel my heart beating?"

She was silent, concentrating on the nerve receptors in her palm. A hard *thump, th-thump* beat against her hand. "Yes."

He kissed her closed eyes. "When I'm with you like this, I feel alive, as if I've been asleep and you wake me, all of me."

She was enchanted by his confession. "It's the same for me."

"Is it?" He leaned away from her to peer at her

intently. "Is this another of your games, Tess? Do you just want to prove your power over me? You can drive me crazy, and you know it."

He spoke with a fierceness that should have been frightening. But she knew this man, better than she knew any other.

With trembling hands, she cupped his face, so dear to her in all its moods and passions. She'd seen him laughing and full of devilment as he teased her. She'd seen him angry, cold and distant. In his eyes, she'd seen desire and she'd seen pain. But she had never seen cruelty, not even when he'd rejected her.

"You have the same power," she replied.

He drew a deep breath, compressing her breasts between them. He looked at the point where they made contact. "Take off your sweater. I want to see you."

When he moved away, she sat up and pulled the garment over her head, giving it a toss to the floor. Her bra followed. She heard him gasp as her breasts sprang erect and free. When he dipped his head and kissed her almost reverently on each raised tip, she clenched her hands in his hair.

He settled against her. He took her lips in a kiss that stopped her breath. Against her, she was aware of his movements as he unfastened his shirt and slipped it off. Then there was flesh on flesh, hot, smooth and exciting. They'd never gotten this far all those years ago. It was ecstasy.

His hands roamed restlessly, touching her breasts, moving on, returning, keeping her on the verge of insanity while his lips pleasured hers with kisses that left her dazed. He explored her mouth thoroughly, making her shiver with a desire for more. She wanted...everything.

With a slight movement, she opened her legs, inviting him within the embrace of her thighs. He pressed against her, the caress of their bodies becoming more intimate. She could feel his hardness against her and wanted all he could give.

"Easy, love," he gasped when she moved against him, giving herself entirely to the passion. Everything disappeared from her consciousness except what was happening between them.

She opened her eyes when he lifted his head to study her face.

"You used to look at me like that," he said hoarsely. "With fire and passion in your eyes. And yet, you were so innocent and trusting. It was like looking into your soul."

"Don't talk," she pleaded. "Not now."

She moved her head restlessly against the sofa pillow. The flash of diamonds sparkled from her ears.

Carson stared at the stones. They were part of a matched set, a gift from her family at her graduation. He'd read about it in the paper. He couldn't afford to give her diamonds, not even tiny ones. So where was this passion leading them?

"I have one question, Tess." He waited for her to look at him again. "You were a virgin then. Are you now?"

She closed her eyes tightly and shook her head.

"I think you're lying."

"No. I swear."

"Look at me."

She opened her eyes.

"You're still as inexperienced as you were at seventeen," he accused softly.

"What does it matter? I want you. Now."

"What about children?" he asked.

"No. It's okay."

He laughed shortly. "I'm a mongrel, Tess. You're a Garrick of the Garrick Valley Ranch. What would your family say?"

"They'd want me to be happy."

"In an affair with a rancher who's probably going to lose his shirt within the next couple of years?"

"It doesn't have to be that way." She caressed his cheek. "I know we can make it—"

He levered himself away from her, fatigue sweeping over his body, taking part of the passion, though not all. As long as she lived and breathed, he'd always want her.

"With your money, Tess?" He deliberately made himself laugh cruelly. "I should marry you and use your money to fix this place up. That would be smart, wouldn't it?"

"So why don't you?" she challenged.

He looked into the future. It was one thing to go down the tubes by yourself; it was another to take someone down with you.

"I have to face myself in the mirror every morning," he replied, and walked swiftly down the hall to his bedroom before he forgot his good intentions. A man had to live with his conscience as well as his desires.

Chapter Seven

Tess mulled over his statement on her way to town Monday morning. His conscience would bother him if he made love to her because he didn't love her and didn't *want* a future for them? Was that what he meant? He'd said once before that it would only be sex between them, but she hadn't believed him. They'd shared something too real five years ago. She wouldn't give up, not yet.

Today was the beginning of the fourth week at Carson's ranch. She'd give herself two more weeks to convince him—just until Dev and Lainie and Davie got home—then she'd redirect her life.

She pressed a hand to her middle, feeling the tightness return as she considered leaving. Every season had its limits, she reminded herself, looking at the buds on the prickly pears. They were evidence that spring was replacing winter. Finally.

In town, she finished her shopping then meandered along the street, looking in the shop windows. She really should get home. This afternoon she planned to start painting the kitchen walls. Rachel and the boys were going to help. She also intended to refinish the kitchen cabinets. At least she'd get that much done before she left. It suddenly seemed important.

Was she trying to leave her imprint on his house since she couldn't seem to make one on his life?

Stopping in front of the hardware and carpet store, she gazed at the shiny patterns of vinyl floorings on display.

A man came up and stood beside her. She looked at his image in the glass. His well-worn Stetson was pushed back on his head. A dark wave dipped roguishly across his forehead, then feathered off to the side.

"Which one would you choose?" Carson asked.

"The one that looks like tiles of honey-colored clay with bits of darker clay ingrained in it." She pointed to the second rack in the display stands. "It'd go well with the curtains."

"What about a countertop?"

She shook her head. "The one at the house is fine." The butcherblock counter in the kitchen looked like dark oak planking.

"Let's get the flooring. It's on sale."

Taking her arm, he guided her inside the store while she stared at him in surprise. "What are you going to use for money?" she whispered when they stopped before the vinyl section.

"The truck account." He grinned insouciantly at her.

"You're using that to pay the Montagnas."

He scowled down at her. "Are we going to have a fight about it right here in the middle of the store?" Dammit, he was trying to apologize for his behavior of last night.

She shook her head and looped a strand of dislodged hair behind her ear. When she glanced at him, he was looking at her hair. The times when he had kissed her he had liked to touch her hair, too. Prickles of remembered ecstasy ran along her scalp.

"What can I do for you today?" Silas, the store owner, asked, coming over and including them both in his question.

Everyone in town knew they were partners, it seemed. Tess wondered what else they thought, then decided it didn't matter.

"We need to replace the kitchen floor," Carson explained. He spoke as if he did this kind of thing regularly. "My partner likes this pattern. How wide does it come?"

The two men decided on the number of square yards needed, and Silas cut it off the huge roll.

"Here, you carry that end," Carson ordered Tess, after paying the bill. "I'll get this one."

Together they toted the rug to the pickup.

"Ready to go?"

She nodded.

"I'll follow you home."

When he saw the Mustang, his eyebrows went up, but he didn't say a word. Tess wished he had. She felt like arguing. The back seat of the car was crammed with plants of all sizes and varieties.

At the ranch house, he helped her bring everything in. "How much do I owe you for the groceries and the greenhouse?" He was being very good-natured about the whole thing. "I'll write you a check tonight."

She told him the amount. "I suppose you think the plants were extravagant," she said, her lips in a belligerent curl.

He stared at her mouth. "No. They look nice."

"Oh. Well, I thought I'd give this palm to Rachel as sort of a housewarming gift." She waited for him to explode.

"Good idea. Any more of those gingerbread cookies left?"

"In the jar."

He took several and walked out.

"One thing for sure—I'll never figure him out," she muttered, and started pacing the plants in various rooms.

Rachel, Richard and the two youngest boys, Benjie and Thomas, came over after lunch. "The boys are now enrolled in school," Rachel announced. "They start next week."

"I'll miss them," Tess admitted. She smiled at Richard, her most stalwart companion, ready to brave pecking hens and kicking stallions with her. She realized she would rarely see the family when she went back to the Garrick spread. "Well," she said huskily, "shall we get started?"

They worked all afternoon, cutting in around the

woodwork and light switches. Tess liked to get the details out of the way, then switch to a roller to finish the walls. She gave the youngsters each a section to paint while she and Rachel completed two walls.

"It's time for you to prepare supper," Tess reminded her helper. "You go on and I'll take care of the cleanup. It only takes soap and water with latex paint."

After the others left, she studied the last two walls. Since she was covering white walls with almond-toned paint, they took one coat. She could roll them and be done in no time.

Carson returned to the house when she was halfway along one wall. He pulled off his boots, perusing her and the room. "You have little splatters of paint all over you."

"It's the roller. It throws out a fine spray," she said, continuing her chore. "I'll be through in about an hour. If you're hungry, there're ham and cheese in the frig."

"Ah, I wondered how long those hot meals would last."

"I'm *painting*," she retorted. She slung the roller down, marched over to the refrigerator and grabbed the ham and cheese from the bin.

Just as fast, he was across the room, taking the stuff from her and tossing it back in. He slammed the door and leaned on it.

Tess glared at him, her hands on her hips. "Is this a fight?" she demanded.

He crossed his arms over his chest. "Maybe."

They eyed each other. Since the previous night,

they'd been stepping around each other like two cats primed for battle.

"State your problem, McCumber," she snapped.

"You."

"So?"

He sighed and pushed himself away from the frig. "I'll help you finish in here." Picking up Rachel's roller, he set to work on the last wall.

Tess went back to her station. "Sometimes I just don't understand men at all," she muttered.

He gave her a hard glance over his shoulder, then attacked the wall, paint flying out in a furious whirl around the roller. "I want to make love to you. What could be simpler than that?" The softness of his tone didn't mesh with the scowl on his face.

"You're throwing more paint around than the kids did," she protested.

"Do you want to do the damned thing yourself?" His glare should have sizzled her hair.

"Did I ask for your help? The least you can do is do it right, if you're going to insist on being the helpful male."

"Hell," he said. "Where's a paint rag?"

She saw that he'd hit the side of the window sill. "Here." She handed him a paper towel. "You don't have to get so close to the woodwork. That's why Rachel and I cut a wide swath around everything."

"Thank you so much, Mr. Mudd." Fritz Mudd was a local painter.

"You're so welcome."

Tess finished first and carried her roller to the sink in the pantry. She washed it and her pan, then checked for any missed spots on the walls before taking up the protective papers from most of the floor. She moved Carson's roller pan closer to his working area, removed the drip cloth from the table and went to the refrigerator, determined to make ham-and-cheese sandwiches.

Carson stepped back from the wall to reload the roller and stepped into the paint.

"Argggh," he roared.

Tess looked around.

He was standing on one foot while he held the other in the air, almond paint dripping from his sock, a look of disbelief on his face. He jammed the roller against the nearest support to stabilize his precarious balance.

"Oh, no," she cried. " Watch out."

It was too late. The roller slipped and a big streak of paint zipped right down the middle of the oak table. Carson landed on the floor, the roller landed next to him...a foot off the paper, naturally.

"I just cleaned and polished that table within an inch of its life last week," she wailed. "And look at the floor."

"Who moved the damned bucket?" A crack of thunder directly overhead couldn't have been louder than his voice.

Tess offered a tentative smile. "I pushed it just a tiny bit closer," she confessed.

"A tiny bit," he echoed. He drummed his fingers on the paint-smeared floor. "It was only a tiny bit," he repeated, sounding as if he were trying to talk some invisible person into a reasonable state of mind. "She only moved the paint a tiny bit. A TINY BIT!"

Tess clutched the cool packages of ham and cheese to her chest, her stance wary of Carson and his eroding temper. She pressed the back of one hand to her mouth. She bit her bottom lip...hard. It was no use. Laughter erupted from her like a cheerful geyser unable to contain itself any longer.

She doubled over and held her stomach. She crammed the ham against her lips. It was no use. The sight of him sprawled on the floor, tiny speckles of paint in his hair, covering his face and work clothes, one sock dripping paint, with the floor and table around him looking like a disaster area, was just too much for her control. She closed her eyes and let the tide of laughter take her.

"How would you like to be covered with paint?" he demanded when she finally wiped tears of laughter from her eyes.

That sent her off again.

A patient smile appeared on his face. He pulled his socks off and tossed them into the sink. Using the dish towel, he wiped up all the paint and threw the towel in the trash. Then without further ado, he finished the wall.

Tess leaned against the counter and watched, her sparkling eyes taking on a wistful glow as she noted the strong movements of his arm and back as he rolled the paint on evenly and slowly.

An hour later they sat down to their sandwiches. Carson had helped Tess finish the cleanup, then they had decided to take their baths before eating. Now they sat across from each other, the curtains restored to the windows, the room a little smelly, but bright and cheerful otherwise.

Tess was in her gown and robe. Carson had on fresh jeans and a blue sweater. She doubted if he slept in pajamas. Most ranchers kept a pair in case they had to go to the hospital, but outside of that, she suspected they wouldn't have been caught dead in sissy things like pajamas.

"Need some aspirin?" she asked, shaking a couple from the bottle for herself. She scooted it across the table.

"No, I'm all right." He frowned slightly. "Are you hurting?"

"Everywhere," she exclaimed dramatically before giving him a contented smile. "Doesn't it look marvelous in here? I can't wait until we get the vinyl laid. I'm going to start on the cabinets tomorrow. Unless there's something else I should be doing?"

"No," he said. "You're doing fine."

"Rachel and I will plant the garden next week."

"Fine."

They finished their supper. It was after ten. A long day. Tess wished she could crawl into bed with him and just snuggle up and go to sleep. She wondered if her wish was revealed in her eyes. For a second she thought she saw a light flare in his, then it was gone.

"Good night," she murmured, and went to bed.

"Okay, girl, you're all through," Tess said, giving Patches an affectionate pat on the neck, then turning to the next stall.

The stallion had watched the proceedings with the mare with an interested air. Since the mating, he'd been more docile, even to the point of following the mare inside the barn and letting himself be coaxed into a large stall.

"Of course, a bucket full of oats helped, didn't it?" Tess grinned at him. She held up a stiff brush. "Want a brushing?"

He sniffed at the brush, then looked at Tess. His gaze was steady, full of intelligence and courage.

"Okay, let's try it," she said. She stood on a stool and leaned over the wooden planking. Gently she set the brush down on the stallion's shoulder. A muscle twitched under his skin, but he didn't back off. With slow, careful movements, she brushed along his back. When he moved closer, she smiled.

Becoming bolder, she hoisted a leg over the plank. The stallion didn't seem to mind. He was enjoying the grooming session too much. After a good fifteen minutes, she lowered herself into his stall, not missing a stroke with the brush and talking in a low croon the whole time. The stallion accepted her.

She brushed him expertly, over his withers and down his shoulders onto his broad chest, along his sturdy barrel of a body to his flanks. He let her touch him without a flicker of fear.

When she tired, she eased past him and out the stall door, her eyes shining. She removed the apple from her jacket pocket. "Here," she said, holding it out. Patches immediately stuck her head over the stall and reached for it. Tess let the mare take the treat. She had another for the stallion.

He hesitated when she held it out for him. Then he danced forward with dainty, mincing steps as if ready to bolt at any moment. With his big front teeth barely touching the apple, he took it from her fingers, then ate it greedily. He stuck his head over the door and looked at her searchingly.

''You big phony,'' she chided, laughing. ''You're as easy to spoil as any male I ever met.''

''Easy with the insults. If he doesn't bite you, I might,'' warned a deep, warm voice behind her.

She turned. Carson was leaning against the stall across from them. ''How long have you been here?''

''Since you decided to try for suicide and climbed in the stall with that beast.'' He recoiled the bull whip he held and hung it back on the wall.

Tess realized he had stayed to protect her. It gave her a warm feeling. They seemed to be on good footing since he'd stepped in the paint and she'd laughed herself silly over it. That had been two evenings ago.

''I'm going into town for some parts for the truck. Do you need anything?'' he asked, falling into step beside her when she slipped into her jacket and started toward the door.

''No, everything's fine. I'm going to work on the cabinets again this afternoon.'' She laughed and went out as Carson held the door open for her. ''It's like going back in time. I've uncovered four different colors of paint on them. They were a sort of ghastly pink before this last coat of white. Before that, they were avocado green—that was a popular color of the fifties, I think—then they were white again.''

''I remember the pink. My mother thought it was

going to turn out a soft tangerine. She made my dad and me repaint them white a week later.'' He chuckled, remembering.

Tess tucked her arm in his as they walked across the muddy ground toward the house. ''The wood is oak. It looks in good shape. I thought I'd stain it, then use a clear varnish to seal it. Is that okay?''

Carson gazed at her questioning face. ''Sure.''

The warmth in his eyes confused her. Before she could react to it, he reached out and touched the end of her nose with one finger, then he laughed. ''See you later.'' He left her at the granite stoop and went to the truck.

Tess stood there for a long minute, watching him drive away. He seemed to be feeling better about the ranch. Actually, things were going well. Since all the accounts were posted and up to date, he had gone over them with her the previous evening.

The final count on the spring crop of beeves was much better than he had anticipated. She had seen the look of relief in his eyes when he had realized his financial position wasn't desperate. Not that it was great, but he had some breathing room. If next year went well, and there was no reason why it shouldn't with Ramon and the boys there to help, well, then...

She daydreamed of the future while scanning the clouds forming over the ridge. Those were thunderheads. There'd be rain before the day was over.

A light drizzle started around three o'clock. Tess yanked off the rubber gloves as she looked out the window. The sky was an angry gray, and the rain would probably keep up for a while. Through the open doors of the storage barn, she could see Carson and the others working on the truck.

Throwing the worn-out gloves in the trash, she stood back to admire her handiwork. The cabinets were stripped bare of their old layers of paint and grime. The grain of the oak was beautiful. Tomorrow she'd stain them and Friday she'd seal them.

The next two days passed in a pleasant haze of work. The rain let up, and Tess decided the humidity was low enough to seal the cabinets. Rachel volunteered to help. By midafternoon they were through. They'd have to wait until the urethane sealer was dry before rubbing it with ultrafine steel wool for a satin finish.

The rain began again that night. Tess turned the heat up to keep the moisture out and to take the chill off the house. Carson had taken the truck to the garage in town for the final part of its overhaul and wasn't back yet.

After eating her solitary supper, she left the beef stew in the slow cooker and retired to the living room. She built a fire and settled on the sofa with a magazine, tired but happy. Two hours later, she snuggled down and went to sleep.

With the drizzly rain still falling, Carson took the paved county road back to the ranch. It was longer than the ridge road, but he was surer of getting home rather than stuck on the back road for the night.

The headlights cut a feeble path through the rain-dark night and he had to concentrate on staying on the road. The pavement wasn't marked with white stripes and it tended to disappear when wet, so it was damned hard to know if he was on the road or not.

Finally he reached the turnoff to his house. Before he climbed the last hill leading down into the small, flat valley where the two houses and buildings were located, he glimpsed a flash of light to the west of him. Must have been lightning, although the storm wasn't a hot one.

At the top of the hill, he saw another flicker of light, not in the sky, but on the ground. He threw on the brakes and hit the light switch. The sudden darkness was absolute, as if a blanket had been thrown over his windshield. He backed up slowly until he was again on the crest of the hill. He waited.

Twin beams of light flashed briefly against the finger of cliff that jutted into the valley. Then all was dark.

Suspicion built like a thunderhead in him. Along with it, fury raged with the turbulence of a wind shear. Easing the truck back into gear, he drove until he was at the bottom of the hill, then he cautiously turned his low beams on and stomped the gas pedal. At the ranch house, he pulled up to the granite slab and dashed inside, leaving the engine running.

After retrieving the key to the gun case from his desk, he flung it open and reached inside. The twelve-gauge gleamed like new in the light of the desk lamp as he shoved a shell into each chamber and stuffed the box into his jacket pocket. He loaded another shotgun and added another box of shells to an empty pocket. Now he was ready to face whatever waited in the south meadow where the main part of his small herd was pastured.

When he turned to leave, Tess stood in the doorway, her eyes wide with alarm. "What is it?" she asked.

"Polecats," he bit out in a snarl. He started past her.

She grabbed his arm. "Tell me the truth."

"There's something or someone over near those cows. I'm going to take a look."

"With two loaded guns?" A light dawned in her eyes. "Rustlers. Wait, I'm coming with you." She preceded him to the kitchen and removed her boots from the bench.

He had no intention of taking her. Before she could get her boots and jacket on, he was off, driving hard through the mist, following a barely discernible dirt road that was rain-slickened and dangerous. When he dropped over the other side of the jutting promontory, he had to zigzag down the steep trail. There was no way he could turn his lights off.

He reached the meadow just as the rustlers pulled out with a tractor-trailer rig filled with his best beef. He gunned the pickup and slewed in front of them, cutting off their escape. The big truck hauled to the right, just missing him. The driver whipped the wheel furiously, heading for the paved road as fast as he could. Carson took off across the rough pasture after him, determined not to let them escape.

In a short distance, he overtook the truck, passed it and again drove directly into its path. The truck came to a stop. A man leaped out the passenger side of the cab and ran toward the pickup. He carried a gun.

Carson was just as fast. ''Don't come any closer,'' he warned. ''I've got you covered.''

The man stopped. From the open window of the truck, he heard the driver curse.

''Put your gun down real slow.''

The man did as told.

''Now let's just move to the back and let those cows loose, then you fellows can leave. Nobody gets hurt that way.''

A light came over the hill, bouncing wildly along the rutted road. Carson groaned inside. He knew who it was.

The Mustang seesawed back and forth along the hairpin turns and streaked across the muddy pasture. It stopped beside the truck, the lights shining in Carson's eyes.

He heard the thief chuckle, saw a motion against the glare, then ducked as a shot was fired over his head. The thief ran to the fender of the truck, taking partial cover there. He aimed his gun directly at Tess when she got out of the car.

''Carson,'' she cried. ''Are you all right?''

''Yeah, your boyfriend's fine, ma'am. Just don't move and you'll be fine, too.'' He laughed. ''Put your gun down real slow, cowboy, and join your lady. We'll just mosey on out of here and not cause you folks any more trouble. Of course, I've got to disable your wheels.''

When Carson stood beside Tess, the rustler drew a knife and hit a tire on each vehicle, then he climbed in the truck and it took off. Carson and Tess stood in the dark, watching the red taillights move away, pause at the junction of the paved road, then turn right and speed out of sight.

"Are you all right?" Tess demanded, her hands reaching for him as if searching for wounds.

"Am I all right? Of course I'm all right. Practically my whole herd of cattle, my entire livelihood, has just been stolen, but why shouldn't I be all right? Dammit, Tess, I had them covered. The guy was in my gun-sights, and then you drive up."

"I was worried—"

"Who needs your worry!" he exploded. He started to shake her, then changed his mind. The way he felt at the moment, he just might strangle her.

Tess felt terrible. Right after she had stopped the Mustang and called out to Carson, she knew she'd played right into the rustlers' hands. When the man by the truck had grabbed the gun from the ground and fired at Carson, she had died a little herself.

"Carson, I'm sorry," she pleaded. "I realized too late what was going on."

He walked away, then spun around. With the lights from her car shining on him, he looked like a demon. "You interfering little busybody. Can't you ever leave well enough alone?"

She bit back the tears. This was no time for crying. "I'll go call the sheriff. I got the license number of the trailer."

"I'll have to change the tires first," he said. He had moved past anger, she saw. Now he was merely weary and resigned.

He went to the pickup and changed its tire. After moving it so its headlights shone on her car, he changed her tire. Without another word between them, they drove to the ranch house. Carson called the sheriff after getting the license number from Tess. She stayed in the kitchen and made a pot of coffee. She had his food on the table when he entered.

He hung his sheepskin jacket on a hook beside her wet one and took off his boots, placing them inside the bench next to hers.

"Do you want milk with your beef stew?" she asked, subdued by the weight of guilt for her part in the rustlers' success. If she hadn't come racing up, he'd probably still have his beeves.

"I don't care."

She poured a glass and watched him eat in a methodical way, his handsome face void of all emotion, even anger. When he finished, she took the dishes away and gave him a slice of pie. He ate it without saying a word. She doubted if he knew what he was eating. He finished and laid the fork down.

"Carson, I'm so sorry."

He looked up at her, hovering so anxiously on the other side of the table. His eyes were as flat as the granite slab outside the door. She wished she could detect something. Even anger would be better than this blankness she witnessed.

He took a deep breath. "Tomorrow I want you out of here. I'll deed you enough acres along the ridge where our land joins to pay off the loan as soon as the courthouse opens in the morning. Then I'll be free of you."

He got up and walked out, going into his office and closing the door. Tess stood as if frozen into a statue.

Tomorrow, she thought. Tomorrow, when he's calmer, we'll talk. He'll listen then. Tomorrow.

She went to bed and spent a sleepless, miserable night. At six, she got up and looked out the window. It was still raining.

Chapter Eight

Carson was in the kitchen when she entered. He was still dressed in last night's clothing. Stubble covered the lower part of his face. He looked as ruthless as a rustler.

He'd made coffee and was now drinking it as he leaned against the counter, watching the rain fall in a steady downpour.

When she walked toward him, he moved aside so she could get a cup of coffee. She poured one, then started to get bacon out of the refrigerator. A strong brown hand clasped her wrist.

"I meant what I said last night. I want you out of here just as soon as you can get packed."

Tess trembled under his touch. His breath caressed her temple when he spoke, and although the words were harsh, she couldn't help reacting to his nearness. She turned, surprising him, and took his face between her cold hands.

"What kind of partner runs out just when the going gets rough," she asked him, teasing but serious. "I want to be here when the police bring those scoundrels in."

He shook his head impatiently. "Don't you ever listen? I said I didn't want you here. You're a distraction I can't afford. My life is complicated enough without you."

She dropped her hands to her side. "Don't send me away just when you need me the most. Let me be your comfort in hard times, just as you'll be mine. Together we can make it, Carson."

He stepped back from her and slid his hands into his pockets. "You just never give up, do you? How do I convince you?" A slow smile spread over his face, chilling her. "But you Garricks never quit until you get what you want. And I know just what you want, don't I, Tess? You've wanted it ever since you were seventeen, but I've not been very cooperative. Sorry about that."

He reached for her, his hands closing on her shoulders to bring her against his chest, then his arms slid around her, holding her so there was no escape. His mouth descended on hers.

She turned her head. "No, Carson, don't," she said as calmly as she could. She didn't believe he would really do what his actions implied, but there was just that one element of doubt. She'd never seen him look so grim and unforgiving.

"Oh, yes, Tess," he muttered, kissing all along her hairline. "We've waited a long time for this, you and I."

"Not this," she whispered. "This is anger, not love."

"Don't use that word," he ordered. "This is sex, an act of the hormones, just like the stallion and the mare. We've wanted each other like this for five years. It's time we...mated."

He took her lips in an endless kiss that demanded her cooperation. She closed her eyes and stood still. Tears seeped from under her lashes like a spring rising out of the granite. She felt cold inside, as if she grieved.

Was he grieving, too?

"Damn you, kiss me," he said. His tongue probed her lips, demanding entry.

"All right," she said. She felt his surprise when she raised her hands and caressed his cheeks, running her fingers over the rough beard on his jaw and along his throat. She lifted her arms and put them around his neck, holding him closer...to comfort him...to comfort them both.

He kissed her without tenderness, without concern for her pleasure, but she didn't fight him. With a sweetness born of despair, she returned every caress, telling him without words of her love for him.

She felt his hand move along her side, come between them to cup her breast and tease the nipple to a hard point. With his other hand, he pressed her hips to his, letting her feel the powerful result of his male passion. She touched him back, always in gentle ways, letting him know of her desire, too.

His belt buckle bit into her skin as he moved to hold her closer still. His heart thudded against her chest, shaking them both. So fierce, her lover, she thought. Tenderness welled up in her, and compassion. He had fought the land and elements alone for five long years. Last night he'd lost the little he'd gained because of her. She longed to repay him for her stupidity.

"I want you," he said. He lifted his head, their breathing rapid, filling the space between them. "Will you come with me?"

"If you want me to."

"To bed."

She nodded.

"There'll be no love words or pretty speeches," he warned. "And when it's over, there'll be no apologies."

"I understand."

His eyes narrowed. A minute passed. Another. She waited.

At last he laughed shortly. "You know I can't do this."

"I'd hoped."

He released her and walked away, running a hand through his hair. "Get out of my life, Tess."

"If I do, you'll lose more than a herd of cows. We had something beautiful all those years ago, something that's lasted, I think." Her voice shook with intensity. She wanted so badly for him to see the life they could share. "We could have it again, Carson. A future. We'd be a family—"

He faced her, his face cold once more. "A family? I can't afford a dog, much less a family. I hope you have room for the Montagnas at your place. I sure as hell don't." He strode to the door. "I have to go to town to file a report. Turn out the lights when you leave."

With that, he was gone.

Tess looked around the kitchen one more time. Soup simmered in the slow cooker. Maybe Carson would learn to use it instead of leaving a pot simmering on the stove.

Although no sunlight came through the windows, the curtains added a warm touch to the room. So did the oak cabinets. She'd taken the time to rub and polish them before packing. When Carson put down the vinyl flooring and installed a new sink, the kitchen would look like something out of a magazine.

The rest of the house, with the profusion of plants she'd added, was tastefully decorated and cheerful. She was satisfied she'd done the best she could.

After checking that the lights were off and the furnace turned to sixty degrees, she closed the door and climbed into the red Mustang. With a quick flip of the switch, the engine started. She had no excuse to delay.

She'd already told the Montagnas goodbye. She'd taken it upon herself to tell them they had a job on the Garrick ranch if Carson couldn't keep them. Sighing, she glanced around the stable yard. She'd send one of the men with a horse trailer for Patches.

"The stallion," she murmured. She'd forgotten all about him. He was in the paddock, his head over the fence, looking at her.

She killed the engine and got out. With a set expression, she went to the gate and opened it.

"Okay, you can go," she called out.

The stallion eyed her nervously, suspicious of her actions. He pawed the ground a bit, then looked at her as if wondering where his apple was. Patches gave a whicker from inside. Carson had told the boys not to turn her out for a few days.

"Get on," Tess cried, exasperated with the stupid animal. "You're free. You can go and do as you damned well please."

The horse shied backward when she went into the paddock. She circled behind him and waved her arms up and down. He circled around, too, and ignored the open gate.

Tess stomped into the stable and grabbed the bull whip. Outside, she dropped the coils and cracked the whip. The stallion reared and stamped. With the second crack, the whip flicked him on his hind quarters, startling him. He moved toward the gate. Tess popped the whip over his back. He darted outside. She closed the gate.

The stallion turned and looked at her. He ran down the road a little ways, then stopped. He called to his mares. Patches answered. Tess heard the mare thump the side of her stall. The stallion shook his mane and danced around in a circle.

"I don't have all day to fool with you." She picked up a rock and threw it at him.

He spun and took off, his tail streaming out behind him. In a minute, he disappeared over the nearest hill.

Tess returned to the car. She cranked it up and

began the long drive home. The ridge road was out of the question in this constant rain. It would be nothing but mud.

At the top of the hill, she caught one more glimpse of the Appaloosa, running free across the range. She watched him as long as she could, until the mist obscured her vision.

Carson found out it wasn't as easy to transfer two hundred acres in fact as it was in words. First the land had to be surveyed and staked out. Next it had to be appraised. Then a lawyer had to draw up a bill of sale and the title to the land checked. All that took time and money. The latter was a problem. He told them to hold up on it until he decided for sure what to do.

He'd spent the rest of the day filling out forms at the sheriff's office and going over his story. Against his will, he'd had to give Tess's name as a witness, even though he'd argued that there was no reason for her to be involved.

"She was there, wasn't she?" the deputy who was taking his statement asked.

"Yes." Carson relived the effect of seeing Tess in danger, standing by her car while a man with no scruples held a rifle on them. She could have been killed.

"She's a material witness then," the deputy said, typing out the report.

Outside the courthouse, Carson had been detained by a local reporter wanting "all the facts." He'd given a succinct account of the theft and taken off for home.

Back at the ranch, he stopped by the Montagnas'

house to tell them he'd have to let them go. There was no way he could pay them. He reluctantly got out of the pickup and knocked on the front door.

Carl ushered him into the house. Rachel set the boys down in the living room in front of their small, ancient TV with orders not to move, then she bustled around the kitchen, making coffee and cutting a pie. Carson and Ramon sat at the kitchen table.

Carson explained the facts to them. "They'll give you a job over at the Garrick place," he added to Ramon, who was slowly shaking his head in a negative direction.

"No," the hired hand said. "We'll stay here."

"We heard about the rustlers on the news this morning. And, of course, Tess called us," Rachel said, setting pie and coffee in front of the men. "Terrible, what people will do nowadays."

Carson stared at the pie. He hadn't eaten lunch or supper, but his stomach felt like a knot of brimstone. Was that the way Tess felt when her stomach burned with tension?

Ramon spoke again, "The boys and I did a count on the herd this afternoon. It's not so bad—"

"Ramon, those cows were your pay for this fall and next year. They were a new truck and equipment, fences, a snow shelter. I can't pay you even the slave wages you're getting now."

"So we work for food and lodging for a while." He shrugged.

Rachel chimed in. "We've lived on beans and rice before. We can do it again. As soon as the garden comes in, we'll have fresh vegetables to eat with plenty to put up for the winter, too. Besides, we're settled here and have no wish to move again. Have no worries about us.''

Carson fought the burning at the back of his eyes. It was hard to take kindness from people, damned hard. ''You'll need lunch money for the boys.''

''School will be out in June,'' Rachel replied calmly, and continued as if the first statement led to the second. ''Carl and George have taken care of the horses tonight, so you don't have to worry about that.''

Carson saw the couple exchange a look and recognized their determination to stay. ''Why won't you go to Tess?'' he tried one last time.

''To work for her would be to accept a charity. The Garrick ranch does not need us. The McCumber ranch does.''

''To work for me is to accept charity, too,'' Carson said with a rueful grin. ''On my part.''

''We want to stay,'' Ramon said. His wife nodded.

There was no reasoning with some folks. The Montagnas were as stubborn as Tess. ''So, one for all and all for one,'' he muttered, and picked up his fork. ''We'll starve together.''

''We'll do fine,'' Rachel corrected.

The rain had let up, but the day was no less gloomy when Carson drove along the rest of the bumpy ranch road to the main house. The windows were dark.

He realized he'd been expecting them to be ablaze with light and to find Tess still inside, stirring something on the stove while a fire burned brightly in the living room hearth. He'd been geared up to argue with her some more.

The house was cold when he entered. He turned the thermostat up to seventy, turned it back down and put a match to the wood already laid in the hearth. Passing by the gun case, he paused.

The dueling pistols gleamed in their velvet case. When his father had died, Carson had had to pay an inheritance tax. The guns had been valued at thirty-five-thousand dollars at the time. They were a rare and perfect set. What were they worth now? Fifty grand? Enough to get his seed herd started again and keep the place going for another year or two. He'd check with a dealer.

He returned to the kitchen and sniffed the air. Something smelled good.

A slow cooker simmered to the brim with soup, thick with meat and vegetables, just the way he liked it. He remembered his dad giving the pot to his mother one Christmas. She'd been pleased. His father had been good at picking out presents.

He picked up a spoon and stirred the soup. Tess's parting gift, he surmised. She'd found soup on the burner the day she'd arrived; she'd fixed him a potful when she left. Thoughtful, generous Tess. He put down the spoon and replaced the lid.

Just for a minute he let himself dwell on the past few days. He'd begun to think they could make it, that there was a brighter side to the future. He'd even let himself dream a little about having Tess there all the time, about them fixing up the place together like she'd said.

What a laugh! The fates were against him. There'd be no wife, no family, no lights in the windows to welcome him home.

Carson turned and walked outside on the granite slab. It was raining again. He lifted his face and felt the coolness on his cheeks. Then he realized there was no one to see whether the moisture on his face was rain or tears.

The next morning when he went to the stable, he found Patches and the stallion gone. He asked Carl about them. The boy shook his head. "I don't know where they are."

"I know," Richard piped up. He was the eyes and ears of the place. "Tess made the big horse leave, even though he let her feed and brush him. She took the whip and ran him off. She was angry. I hid behind the stable until she drove away." The boy's eyes were round with worry. "Some men came with a trailer and got the other one in the afternoon. They said she sent them."

Carson nodded. "Well, let's get to work. We've got fences to mend and cattle to brand."

His one comfort was that the thieves had taken cows already branded. That gave him a slim chance against the odds of recovering the beasts.

Tess signed the last check and stuck it in the envelope. After sealing it, she laid it with the stack on the corner of the desk and put the ranch books away. Everything was in order. All the accounts were posted, ready for Dev to inspect upon his return.

The family was due back on Monday, only one week away. Maybe the weather would clear up before they returned. Fair weather would be a nice homecoming present.

When they returned, she was going to have to come to a decision about her life. She was a partner with Lainie in the gift shop in town. She might move to the apartment over the store and manage it. She liked doing that sort of thing, and she was good at it. A natural-born manager, Lainie had said. Bossy, some people would say.

A picture of Carson popped into her head.

Poor Carson, she'd about driven him crazy. Hadn't she learned anything when she was seventeen and he'd rejected her then? Apparently not. But she understood the realities of life now, she reflected. A one-sided love was the same as no love at all.

The too-ready tears pricked the backs of her eyelids, but she refused to give in to them. She'd cried last Thursday all the way home from the McCumber ranch to the Garrick spread. No more tears.

Gathering the mail, she put the envelopes in her purse. "Rose, I'm off to town. Anything else we need? I've got the grocery list."

"Tess, come listen to this," Rose cried.

Tess ran down the hall from the office to the kitchen. The radio was on.

"...Recovered the McCumber herd last night. The officers making the arrest grew suspicious when the men hurriedly left the truckstop without eating their meal when the troopers arrived."

"It's about Carson McCumber," Rose said excitedly. "They've arrested the men who stole his cattle. In Texas."

"Although the license plate had been changed, the truck matched the description broadcast by the Arizona highway patrol. The officers were further alerted by the clean plate while the rest of the truck was covered in mud. There has been no rain in the Texas area in over a month. The three men are identified as..."

"Three? There were only two men," Tess said. "These may not be the right ones."

"They could have picked up a hitchhiker," Rose suggested. "Or he was an accomplice waiting somewhere else. I know. He was the lookout up by the main road."

"That's possible. Well, I'm off. See you this afternoon. I'm going to stop by the shop and go over the invoices. The accountant was supposed to pay the bills, but I'd better check to see that he did."

She climbed in her old red Mustang and headed for town. The sun was trying to break through the overcast. She was ready for some sunshine. Although the days were warmer, the weather hadn't improved much since spring had arrived a month ago.

Finally, unable to concentrate on the weather anymore, she thought of Carson. She was glad for him. Everything seemed to be working out okay. She'd spoken briefly over the phone with Rachel, who told her that Carson had agreed that they could stay even though he couldn't pay them.

Today Tess was able to admit his acquiescence hurt. If the Montagnas could stay, why couldn't she?

Because he didn't want her. It had taken a long time for the message to get through her thick head, but now she had it.

When she arrived in town, she went by the gift shop. An hour later, she was through. After looking over some new stock, she headed for the grocery. There, she quickly ran her shopping cart up and down the aisles and picked up the items on her list.

By the time she got the bags stowed in her car, it was past one o'clock. She was hungry. Looking over the grocery list, she decided she had nothing that wouldn't keep. She'd go to Nells' for a late lunch.

She wished she hadn't the minute she walked in the restaurant. The noontime rush was over and only a few tables were occupied, one of them by Carson.

He stood as soon as he saw her. When he indicated a chair and raised his eyebrows, she had to accept the nonverbal invitation or look foolish in front of old Mrs. Vickers, the town gossip, who was sitting with her daughter-in-law and giving the poor girl a lot of advice she probably didn't need.

Putting on a nonchalant smile, Tess threaded her way among the tables and took the offered seat. "Hello," she said, "I heard some good news about you this morning. Is it true?"

"I hope so," Carson replied.

She gave him a questioning glance before perusing the menu.

"I haven't seen the cows yet," he explained. "I don't think I'll believe it until I do. They're due back here today. That's why I'm waiting in town. To identify the cattle and the thief who shot at me."

"I see." That was the longest explanation she'd ever heard from him. "What about the driver and the other man the news report mentioned?"

He shrugged. "I didn't get a look at the driver's face. If there was a third man, I didn't see him at all."

"Me, either," Tess said. "I think I can identify the driver, unless he's shaved his beard and mustache. He was fat. When he grinned, his cheeks bulged out. He was smiling when the other man threatened to shoot us."

Carson cursed under his breath, wiped his mouth and threw the napkin in his plate. "You could have been killed," he said with more than a hint of exasperation.

So he still hadn't forgiven her for interfering. She refused to let it hurt or to apologize again. Her concern for him had overshadowed all else. "So could you."

He gave her a hard look, which she returned without flinching. When the waitress brought her water and took her order, Tess had a sense of déjà vu. Well, she was back to square one with the tough, silent cowboy across the table. Only this time, she knew there was no future for them. He'd made that clear enough.

"What is it?" Carson asked.

"What?" She snapped out of her internal musings.

"Is your stomach hurting?"

She realized she'd placed a hand against her middle, a sort of reflex action, she realized, when life didn't go to suit her. "Not really," she answered.

"I've found out it's not what happens to you, but how you react to it that causes the problem. I've decided to stop reacting."

He cocked one eyebrow in disbelief. "To all stimuli?"

"To those that bother me."

"Such as?" His voice dropped to a low, intimate tone.

Was he being deliberately provocative? "It's really none of your business," she said coolly.

He looked taken aback. She was pleased. Just play it cool and nothing can hurt, she advised. She was doing well.

"About the loan..." he started, taking a new tack.

"Yes?"

"It's a hassle signing over the acreage. Unless you insist, I'll pay the interest this year and maybe a little on the rest. Is that okay?"

"Sure. If the rates fall another whole point, it would be to your advantage to take out a bank loan and pay this one off. That would save you money." She was full of helpful advice, just as he'd been the other time they'd eaten in here. She thought she was being entirely reasonable and controlled. However, his face looked like an Arizona thunderhead ready to crack.

"Maybe I'll do that," was all he said.

"Good."

Her salad arrived and she concentrated on it as if she were going to write up a restaurant review for the paper.

The sheriff came in. Ed stood six six in his stocking

feet and weighed a hefty two-hundred-fifty pounds. He was enough to scare most wrongdoers into going straight. Tess had been terrified of him when she was younger. She smiled as he came over.

"The truck is here," he said, tipping his hat to Tess and speaking to Carson. "They're your beeves, no doubt about it. The rustlers didn't change the brand, but they had irons with them."

"I'd like the names of those Texas Rangers," Carson said. "I'll send them a reward."

"A pretty thank-you card would be enough. They were just doing their job. Can't take a reward for that," Ed advised dryly. "You two were sure lucky."

"How's that?" Carson asked.

"From what one of the men said, the third hombre was in the back of the truck. If you forced the other guy to open the doors, he was going to shoot you."

Tess wondered if she had turned white. The news had stunned her. "Why didn't they shoot us anyway?" she asked.

The sheriff grinned. "It was bad enough when one person caught them. When you come tearing down the road, too, they didn't know how many others might be on the way. They hadn't counted on fighting off the entire county and only had three guns."

"*Only,*" Tess muttered.

Carson grinned slightly. "The odds were three to two in their favor, if they'd only known."

"Two?" Ed asked, glancing at Tess as if he didn't think she counted for much.

"I had another gun with me. Fat lot of good either one of them did me, though."

Tess looked down at the paper place mat. If she hadn't driven up like a dumb heroine in a B Western, Carson would have nabbed the thieves right then, instead of having to go through all this worry for five days.

"Well, all's well that ends well, as somebody once said," Ed declared. "I'll let you get on with your meal. Stop by the office later and I'll sign your cattle over to you so you can take them home. Don't eat 'em, though. They're evidence."

Chuckling over his joke, he waved a hand and left the restaurant. Silence descended like a wet pall.

"I guess I should apologize again," Tess said at last. "I really ruined everything for you, didn't I?"

"Are you being facetious?" Carson demanded, a heavy frown slashing a line between his dark eyes.

"Why should I be?"

He laughed suddenly, confusing her. "I'm sitting here trying to think of a way to thank you for saving my life, and you're apologizing to me." His tone was one of irony.

"What are you talking about?" She felt more than a little irritable. He seemed to see something she didn't.

"Didn't you hear what Ed said? The third man was going to blow me away when I opened the back of the truck to let the cows out. If you hadn't arrived and stopped me, I'd have been buzzard bait by now."

Tess thought back over the events of the dangerous night and what the sheriff said. "One man shot at you anyway. Because of me. I know my car lights blinded you and gave him a chance to retrieve his gun. I realized all that after it was over and they were driving away."

"Let's just say we're even, huh?" he suggested.

His gaze roamed her face, skimming over her forehead, her eyes and finally her lips. She wished he'd leave. The tears pressed behind her lashes and she was afraid that he might sense them. Ah, the sadness of unrequited love, she mocked her emotions, trying to put it all into perspective. She'd live.

Her food arrived. "You don't have to stay," she said with a friendly smile. "Ed will be expecting you—"

He gave her one of his unreadable glances. "Once, you wanted me to stay with you."

The tears surged closer to the surface. *Keep it light.* She wrinkled her nose at him in playful dismay. "The trouble with a small town is that everyone remembers your youthful indiscretions," she complained. "Give me a break."

Carson settled back in his chair, one elbow resting on the table, and studied her thoroughly while she tried to eat and look unconcerned.

"Don't be cynical," he snapped.

"Don't be a hypocrite," she retorted.

That brought a rather astounded expression to his face before he hid behind his granite mask. She considered throwing a glass of water at him and decided against it, not due to fear of his retaliation, but because of Mrs. Vickers, who had watched all the activity at their table. Tess wouldn't give the old biddy an item to work into her snippets of gossip on local affairs.

Affairs. That was a laugh. She and Carson had never had anything so serious and dignified as an affair. She'd just run after him like a puppy at his heels.

"Care to explain that?" he invited in a soft, dangerous tone.

Tess patted her mouth and pushed her plate back, the food hardly touched. Her smile was so forced, she wondered why her face didn't crack. "You made it plain my company wasn't to your liking, ol' love, so consider this an end of it." She dug a crumpled bill out of her jeans pocket. It was a twenty. She dropped it on the table. "Lunch is on me. You paid last time. *Now* we're even."

She walked out. Not one tear fell until she was well out of town. Score one for Tess, zero for Mrs. Vickers.

Chapter Nine

The stallion trumpeted from the hill near the stable. He reared and pawed the air. Against the dawn sky, he looked like a painting, the *Spirit of Freedom*, Carson thought.

Boldly, the horse raced down the hill and right into the stable yard. He whickered softly and nosed around the paddock where Patches used to be. The other two mares answered from inside the building, sounding nervous and anxious.

Carson grinned sardonically. "The one you want isn't here, old chump. She's at her place. You'd probably be shot if you stuck your nose over the ridge."

So would he. Tess would probably do the shooting. He'd seen her in town on Saturday and she'd smiled and nodded as if she hardly knew him. Her family had been with her, home from Hawaii and looking fit. They'd all been talking and laughing.

The stallion gave a bellow of anger and banged the gate a time or two. Carson picked up an apple from the table, went to the back door and threw it across the yard. It landed near the Appaloosa, who sniffed it suspiciously, then daintily picked it up and chomped on it.

"You're spoiled," Carson called to him.

The horse walked over to the granite slab. Carson rubbed its ears. "You're lonely," he added, realizing the truth. Horses were social animals. Like people.

He slapped the stallion on the neck. "Get out of here. I got work to do."

The horse charged off, raced to the top of the hill, whirled and nickered at him. Carson returned to the house. His feet were frozen from standing in his socks on the granite.

The house was totally, eerily silent. It had been for over a week. Since Tess left. A little over a week and it seemed a month or more. Everyday when he came in, he expected to see the lights on, her in the kitchen. Where the hell was she?

The stallion called to his favorite mare again, wanting her with him.

"Face it, fellow," Carson advised. "She's not coming back."

He pulled on his boots, put his cup in the sink with the other dishes that were accumulating, turned off the light, grabbed his jacket and hat and started to work. He couldn't stand around mooning about stupid things all day. In another couple of minutes, the sun would be over the horizon.

The wind cut through him as he walked to the stable. He welcomed the warmth inside the building. He fed the horses and decided to leave them in their stalls today.

The weather had been clear for a week, but during the night a cold wind had started blowing. Clouds were gathering on the ridge to the west. Another storm brewing. Rain, sleet or hail? he wondered. It was going to be a wet, cold spring. What had happened to the global warming trend he'd read about?

He made sure his rain gear was on his saddle before heading for the ridge. He'd seen a weak spot in a fence a few days ago and some cattle over that way. He wanted to drive the cows back this way and check out the fence. Wire cutters, mending wire, pliers, a candy bar—he'd need that for energy before the day was over. The equipment for a quick repair was accounted for. He swung into the saddle and headed out.

Within the first thirty minutes, he was pelted with hail the size of his thumb. Pulling the gelding under a thick canopy of trees, he waited out the flurry. When it stopped, the ground was white, as if covered with snow.

Three hours later he pulled out the candy bar and tore the paper off. He was hungry. The rain had held off until a few minutes ago. Now it fell in a steady drizzle that was mostly annoying. He'd had to stop and put on his slicker.

After tying his horse to a tree, he sat on a cushion of pine needles and watched the fine downpour. The branches above him were thick enough to keep him dry. Sticking one hand in his pocket to keep it warm, he devoured the rest of the candy bar and thought of the pot of soup at the house. Bean soup today with a big piece of ham from the freezer, thanks to Tess.

Don't think about her.

It was damned hard. More and more, she seemed to represent everything warm and good in life. All the things he'd dreamed of accomplishing didn't seem so important anymore. Oh, he still wanted to get the ranch back to its former well-oiled operation, but it was no longer enough. There was more to life.

He stuck the candy wrapper in his pocket and climbed back onto the saddle. The rain had turned partly to sleet. It wasn't a fit day for man or beast, as his mother used to say. He'd go back to the house and catch up on his reading. Thanks to Tess, he didn't have any accounts to do. She'd left everything in order.

Tess. He thought of her lying on the sofa, the firelight reflecting from her hair and eyes, her skin all golden and warm. Honey-girl, sweet and giving when they'd made love.

He was no longer cold. Thinking of Tess warmed him better than a wood-burning stove. He laughed at his longings. The sound came out harsh and cynical. He'd had her there, and he'd sent her away. No use in thinking about it.

Spurring the gelding to a faster pace, he rode through a rock outcropping and up on the ridge. Below him, nestled in a bowl probably carved by glaciers, was a lake, full from the snowmelt and recent rains. From there, on a clear day, he could see the huge Garrick spread, nestled into its rich valley with the creek running through it.

He couldn't see it now, but he knew the creek was running high, right up to the top of its banks. The livestock would be feeding on the new spring growth in all the fields. Tess would be curled up before a fire with a book.

Dammit, don't think about her.

Turning the gelding, he started for home. From the edge of his vision, he saw something not quite right. He looked back. A new creek ran down the western slope of the ridge. A creek?

He looked again. A pounding started in his blood a second before his consciousness recognized the truth: the natural earthen dam that formed the far side of the lake was leaking.

Even as he watched, a piece of sodden earth broke free and tumbled down the steep bank, taking rocks and a shrub with it.

If the dam broke, the Garrick place would be flooded. If that whole side of mud and stones came crashing down, buildings would be torn from their foundations and split into matchsticks. People would die.

With a shout, he wheeled the gelding about and set a furious pace down the western ridge trail, using his spurs whenever the horse faltered. The gelding rolled his eyes as if his master had turned into a madman, and ran down the narrow switchback trail as fast as he could.

Tess looked up from her magazine. Little balls of hail hit the windows of the ranch office with a chattering noise like old bones shaking. She rose, stretched and added a log to the fire.

Nothing like hail, sleet and rain to start a Monday off right, she thought. She had done her chores in the stables as quickly as possible that morning. The wind was cold enough to frost a pumpkin, and she had felt tired and achy. Maybe she had a cold coming on. She'd decided to stay in while Lainie and Dev went to town. Davie was with Rose over at the bunkhouse. He was helping her cook dinner for the hands, a job that seemed likely to be hers for as long as she wanted it.

Tess glanced at the clock. Speaking of cooking, she hadn't eaten anything yet and it was past noon.

After eating a sandwich, she returned to the office, stoked the fire again and settled into a corner of the sofa. Forty years from now, she'd probably still be doing the same. Tess, the old maid.

A commotion at the back of the house had her up and running to see what was wrong. A cowhand rode into the yard, his horse kicking up divots of grass. Lainie wouldn't like that. The man shouted something, but the wind snatched the words away. A shiver ran along her spine. One of the men must have gotten hurt.

She pulled on her boots, sheepskin jacket and a rain poncho. Opening the door, she ran toward the bunkhouse where the horseman had pulled up. She recognized the gelding.

Her heart began to beat with dread.

When she saw the rider was Carson, she breathed

easier. He wasn't hurt. But one of the Montagnas might be. She raced into the bunkhouse.

Carson turned to her from Rose, who was standing next to the stove with a fork in her hand looking helpless. Four-year-old Davie looked from one adult to another.

"Where are your men?" Carson demanded. "The water is breaking through the bank up at the ridge lake. There'll be flooding for sure, maybe a mudslide. You've got to evacuate. Where's Garrick?"

"He's in town." Tess dashed to the wall phone. "I'll call the sheriff. He'll find Dev—"

"Tell him we need men, sandbags—"

"I will," she said.

"Are your hands close to the house?"

"Most of them are working in the south pasture. Blow the horn outside the door, three blasts at a time. They'll know it's an emergency and come right in."

"All right." He went outside.

"Ed? This is Tess Garrick," she said into the phone. "We have an emergency out here." She told him the problem. He promised to find Dev and to round up volunteers.

A tug on her sleeve brought her attention downward when she hung up.

"Aunt Tess, are we gonna die?" Davie asked, his eyes round with fright.

She scooped him into her arms. "No, love, but our house could be ruined if the mud comes down on it."

"You're not supposed to get mud in the house," Davie whispered.

"Well, we're not going to let it get in if we can

help it.'' She gave him a kiss and set him on his feet. ''Rose, we're going to need tons of coffee and sandwiches, hot soup, anything else you can think of. It's going to be a long day.''

''No problem. Davie and I'll get started.''

''If you hear the Klaxon, get in the car and drive like hell for the hill on the other side of the creek. That should be safe.''

''Where will you be?''

Tess grinned. ''Right where Carson doesn't want me, in the thick of things. See you later. Bye, love, and do what Rosie tells you, you hear?''

''I will,'' David said importantly.

Tess exchanged bear hugs with him and headed outside.

Men were pouring into the muddy stable yard in answer to the alarm. She glanced at the barn and had an idea. Laying a hand on Carson's arm, she told him, ''There's a wagonload of hay in the barn. Could we use that as a start?''

''We might,'' he said, frowning as he thought. ''We really need sandbags to plug the crack, though.''

''I know where some burlap bags are. Take a team of men and shovels up to the lake and start filling the bags there. Would that work?''

''Damn right,'' he said, his face brightening. He touched her forehead. ''Good thinking, Garrick. Get those bags. I'll round up the men. We'll need a truck—'' He was off at a sprint.

''Thanks, McCumber,'' she said softly. She went into the stable and gathered up a pile of feedbags. She rounded up all the heavy burlap sacks she could find.

When she went out, Carson and Zed had a tractor hitched to the load of hay and several men aboard. She tossed the bags up and climbed up.

"Stay here, Tess," Carson ordered. "This is no place for you." His frown was forbidding.

She wanted to argue. After all, it was her ranch. Instead she hopped off the wagon. "I'll see about food," she said.

The tractor took off, Zed at the wheel, Carson perched on a fender, directing him. She squinted up at the ridge. The rain was coming down heavier. Could they get there in time?

Returning to the kitchen, she and Davie made sandwiches while Rose fixed gallons of soup. They looked as if they were preparing for a siege. An hour later, Tess was sure of it.

Dev and Lainie arrived home. Behind them were half the town, volunteers from the fire department and other ranchers who'd heard the news. Tess explained the situation.

"I'm taking sandwiches and coffee up to the men now," she told them.

"I'll go with you," Lainie offered.

"Good," Dev said. He and Ed went into the bunkhouse kitchen to plan the best use of the volunteers.

When Tess finally made it up the steep grade in the ranch pickup, she and Lainie were both tired from the tension of the dangerous drive. They jumped out and carried the food up the rest of the way.

Carson and another man were toting a bag of gravel to the base of the earth dam. They placed it on top of another bag. Tess felt her spirits sink when she saw how high the bank was and realized how many bags it would take to shore it up.

"Food," she called. "Take a break. Another crew is on its way. They'll be here shortly."

Carson sent half the men over. The others he kept working on filling bags and stacking them. After all the men had been fed, he stalked over, his face dark with anger. He pushed a wet lock of hair out of his eyes.

"Did your brother know you were driving up here?" he demanded.

Tess was taken aback by his fury.

"Of course," Lainie answered before Tess could gather her wits. Lainie's calm manner was meant to be soothing.

Tess tossed her a grateful smile. Not that she needed defending to this…this tyrant.

"I can't believe any man in his right mind would send two women up that trail," he bit out.

Tess drew herself up to her full height. She and Lainie exchanged glances. Lainie's asked, *Can you handle this?* Tess's answered, *You bet I can!* With a smile, Lainie got in the truck, started the engine and drove off.

"What the hell?" Carson snapped, staring after the truck in disbelief.

"She's going after more coffee. The men will need it." Tess turned on him. "And, yes, my brother is in his right mind. I don't know how you run things at *your* place, but at *our* place, everyone pitches in and helps." She stalked off.

Going to the rocky slope where the two men were

filling bags, she knelt beside them. "Here, I'll hold it open for you." She held the mouth of the sack while the cowhands filled it with rocks.

Carson, after giving her one last scrutiny, returned to his chore. She watched his muscles strain when he and the other man lifted the heavy bag, carried it to the bank and laid it in place. Zed and another man were right behind them. She worried about Zed doing such hard work. After all, he wasn't as young as he used to be. She glanced at Carson. But then, who was?

"Heavens, I'm tired." Lainie pushed her hands against the small of her back and stretched. Her back creaked in a dozen places. She and Tess laughed.

It was ten o'clock. The men had worked all day and into the night, shoring up the soft bank of the lake. Now a sturdy dam of sand and rocks, layered with cement to bind it together, reinforced the earthen dam made by nature.

Out in the stable yard, the last of the trucks arrived, bringing down the last load of weary volunteers. In the bunkhouse kitchen, which could hold fifty in a pinch, every chair was taken as the men ate hearty bowls of soup and wolfed down homemade rolls stacked with meat and cheese.

The rest of the workers came in. They found pegs to hang their hats on. All the cowboys, Tess knew, took their hats off to eat and, she assumed, to sleep. She remembered how neat Carson was in the house. A nice trait in a man.

Dev and Zed set up card tables and chairs to accommodate the crowd. In spite of blisters, caked mud and aching muscles, the men were in good spirits. They'd fought the battle and won, at least for now. The kitchen was filled with laughter and good-natured taunts.

"Ya shoulda seen ol' Jim-Bob here filling them bags with rocks when the new crack opened up," one of the men teased. "He was faster than a steam shovel. Hey, boss, you think we could rent him out to the copper mines?"

"Not a bad idea," Dev called back. "Might make enough to buy the boy a real horse."

The men guffawed. Jim's pride and joy was his cow pony named Good Boy—a meaner, sorrier-looking animal Tess had never seen. It also won all the cattle-cutting contests at the rodeos. She laughed with the rest over the jesting.

Her eyes met Carson's. He was smiling, too, but she didn't think his whole attention was on the conversation. Several times she had seen him watching her and Rose and Lainie going about their chores. He seemed to find it fascinating.

"I'm off," Lainie said. "Sure you don't mind finishing up alone?" Rose had left a few minutes earlier.

"You go ahead. You've done enough."

"And you haven't?" Lainie teased.

Tess tossed her head. "Youth has its advantages." She grinned at Lainie's grimace.

"Don't remind me." She went over to pick David up from the pallet where he'd fallen asleep. Dev was at her side in a second, a mock-ferocious look on his face as he scolded her for not calling him. He scooped his son up as if he hadn't been lifting two-hundred-pound bags of rocks for hours. The three of them left.

Tess watched them go. Someday she'd have a love like that, she vowed. When the door closed, she turned back to her chore of loading the big dishwasher. She glanced at Carson.

He was still watching her, his face as unreadable as a wall of granite. She smiled at him, too tired to react to his hostility or whatever it was he felt toward her.

When he rose to leave, she hurriedly crossed the room. "Carson. I wanted to thank you for warning us about the lake and for helping out."

He raised one eyebrow. "What kind of neighbor would I be if I hadn't?" he drawled.

"You could have just called," she said, refusing to let him denigrate his part in the success of the day. "But you didn't. You came over and pitched right in. Do you have blisters?"

Before he could withdraw, she lifted one of his hands. It had an angry cut on the palm, but no blisters.

"How did you do this?" she asked. "Come, let me treat it."

He pulled his hand away. "It's nothing. I did it on a rock. It'll be okay."

"It looks red already—"

"I'll put some antibiotic cream on it." He picked up his hat and coat and went out the door.

It wasn't until she heard the sound of hooves on the gravel road that she remembered he had ridden his horse. She grabbed her jacket and was out the door in a flash.

"Carson, wait!" she called. She ran to the truck and overtook him. "Put your horse in the stable. I'll take you home."

"I'll ride," he said. "The moon is out now. The trail is bright enough and quicker than going by road." He tipped his hat and set the gelding to a gallop.

Tess watched him go, her pride shredded by his eagerness to get away from her.

Tess studied herself in the mirror. Her dress was golden, pure shining silk, and it clung to every curve of her figure. "Not bad conformation, if I do say so myself," she approved.

There was a grimness in her eyes that was new and a stubborn set to her chin that wasn't. Today she was determined to be the poised, carefree Tess Garrick, heiress and pampered darling of the Garrick Valley Ranch. She would be charming, she would be jolly, and she'd have fun if it killed her.

Today she and Dev and Lainie were throwing a big family-style cookout to welcome spring—now that it had finally decided to arrive—and to thank their friends for the help last month during the emergency. The whole county would probably turn out for it.

Would Carson?

She smiled with little humor. She hoped so. She wanted him to see her. Was she being petty? Yes, but her pride demanded that she let him see she wasn't mourning her lost love.

Like a flash flood, tears filled her eyes, startling her.

That would not do, not at all. Sangfroid, that was what she was aiming for. The cool Miss Garrick.

The emotion passed. She slipped into three-inch heels dyed to match her dress, and pinned a deep gold rose in her hair.

She went downstairs and out on the patio. Everything was ready. Tables already loaded with food were placed into a U-shape. The slam of a car door announced the arrival of their first guests. She went to greet them. When the Montagnas arrived, she introduced them to Dev and Lainie. All five boys came with them.

Two hours later Tess wiped her mouth on her napkin and laid her fork on her plate. "I can't eat another bite," she declared to some old school chums, who shared the table with her.

A group of musicians tuned their instruments in the shade of the bunkhouse porch. There would be dancing soon on a plank floor hammered together for the occasion and a big bonfire later with marshmallows to roast. Everyone was having a good time.

"Dance, Tess?" Robbie Moreley, her classmate and neighbor on the west side, asked. The neighbor who lived to the east of them hadn't attended.

"Sure. I need some exercise after all that food."

"You should worry," Anna Jacobs complained. "You still look wonderful." Anna was married and in her second pregnancy.

Tess smiled over Robbie's shoulder as he led her onto the makeshift dance floor. Would Anna believe Tess would give her yearly allowance to change places with her? Probably not.

The strain of smiling made her mouth tired. Tomorrow she'd take a lunch and ride up into the hills and spend the day by herself. In September she was going to move to town and take over the operation of the gift shop. Lainie was pregnant again, and Dev was determined she was going to take it easy.

When the dance number ended, Robbie leaned her into a dip, her hair brushing the floor as she let her head fall back. When he brought her upright, she looked past Robbie into dark eyes...*black as sin and twice as tempting,* she thought.

He was dressed in black slacks and a white shirt with the sleeves cuffed a couple of times. He wore the Snowy River hat that she loved and his dress boots.

For a second her smile trembled on her lips, then she steadied it. Deliberately, provocatively, she winked at Carson. "Thanks for the dance, Robbie," she murmured, then walked away.

Carson watched her come toward him, all golden radiance, like some kind of magic swan. Her dress drifted around her knees with every step, shimmering in the last rays of the sunset.

Her smile was...devilish, he decided. Her eyes, outlined with color that gave them mysterious depths, issued a challenge. She stood in front of him.

"Dance?"

He nodded.

She turned without looking to see if he followed. He did. He doubted he could have stopped if someone had held a gun on him. Right now his need to hold her was more important than his life.

When she reached the dance floor, she spun gracefully and held up her hands. He stepped forward and took her in his arms.

All around them, he could feel the stares of their friends and acquaintances. There'd be gossip and speculation running like wildfire through the crowd. His eyes met Dev's. Carson nodded solemnly at the other man. Once, they'd almost fought over this golden women he held in his arms.

He hadn't been able to stay away from her when he'd been twenty-three. He couldn't at twenty-eight, either. The battle had been fierce, but after the Montagnas had left to come to the festivities, the ranch had been too silent. He'd had to come.

Just to make sure she was all right.

She looked…beautiful? Self-assured? Rich?

All of the above.

"How's your stomach?" he asked, a brilliant question.

Her eyes flashed. He thought she wasn't going to answer, but then she said, "Fine." Her voice was as cool as a mountain spring.

A picture of her face that night a month ago when she'd offered to drive him home, tired and tinted a ghastly shade from the green lights on the dash of the truck, appeared in his mind. It wasn't the green glow of her skin he saw. It was her eyes.

There had been concern in them when she stopped beside him. She'd been willing to brave both the drive over the ridge to take him home and the return trip alone. When he'd refused her offer, there had been a second of raw pain before her face had closed. That was what had haunted him, why he had to see if she was okay.

Now here he was, holding her, but not in the manner he wanted to hold her. God, she was so lovely, he could hardly breathe.

Diamonds sparkled in her ears and at her throat. He wanted to take them off and kiss her in those places. He pictured her in front of the fire at his house, just the two of them. He would slowly remove her clothing, savoring each delightful sight as he stripped her completely, one item at a time.

"Don't," she said, giving him a repressive glance.

He realized he was caressing her back, the warmth of her skin coming through the cool silk of her dress, tantalizing him with images he couldn't suppress.

"Sorry." His voice was husky with desire.

Tess tried to ignore the message in his eyes, the longing in his voice when he spoke. It called up a wildness of spirit in her. She needed to respond to him as a woman responds to a man.

Never, she vowed. She'd never open her heart to Carson McCumber again. She would not let herself answer the subtle invitation in his dark eyes, not when she'd finally managed to put all that youthful nonsense behind her. She was going to be practical and hardnosed about life from then on.

She wanted a husband, yes, and a family. She'd have them. But she'd choose the man with great care. She'd weigh him and take his measure. If he didn't add up to what she wanted, she'd find someone else.

Marriage would be much simpler if viewed as a contract in which two people received a mutual benefit. She'd be very careful about her choice of partner.

Wasn't that song ever going to be over? It seemed as if they'd been dancing for hours. Just when she was ready to walk off, the music ended. She smiled at Carson, much as she had earlier, letting herself flirt, knowing it meant nothing.

"If you keep that up," he growled near her ear. "I'm going to kiss the living devil out of you right here in front of everyone."

"My brother would beat you up," she said, dismissing his threat.

She glanced over her shoulder at Dev. He wasn't paying the slightest attention to them. Mrs. Vickers was, though.

"I think not," Carson said.

"Why do you say that?"

"You're a woman now. You can take care of yourself."

She was surprised at his tone. He was smiling as if he were joking, but his eyes were serious. She gave up trying to figure him out. It took too much energy. "Kind of you to notice."

"I noticed." His eyes swept over her. "I'm hungry. Have you eaten yet?"

She nodded. Her hair bobbed around her shoulders.

"Join me while I eat." He took her elbow and headed for the tables, which were steadily replenished as soon as the food disappeared.

Tess withdrew her arm. "No, thank you. I think I'll rejoin my friends. We're having a sort of class reunion, catching up on everyone and all that. Good night."

Holding her head erect, she returned to her place beside Anna.

"Are you two still partners?" Anna asked.

Tess watched Carson speak to Dev and Lainie. His smile was devastating, enough to break any young girl's heart who was foolish enough to let it. He left the party without saying goodbye.

"Tess?" Anna said.

Tess turned to her friend. "No, we're not partners. We never were, not really."

"You used to be crazy about him when we were in high school. I suppose that's all over. Teenage romances rarely last, except in special cases." With a tender smile, Anna looked across the table at her husband, who had been her high school sweetheart.

Tess took a cooling drink of punch. "Yes, it's all over."

Chapter Ten

The stallion nickered. Carson went to the kitchen door and tossed an apple out. The Appaloosa caught it in midair.

"Show-off."

Carson let the screen door bang shut behind him and headed for the coffeepot. He poured another cup and leaned against the counter, watching the stallion roam the stable yard. At the moment, it was checking out his stock. It rubbed noses with the mares, then looked the gelding over as if deciding whether to challenge it.

Suddenly the stallion turned, galloped off a short distance, turned again and charged the fence. It sailed right over the top rail without touching it.

Carson nearly spilled hot coffee down his shirt front.

The horse nuzzled the two mares, then walked over

to the pile of alfalfa hay in the corner and began munching.

"Well, I'll be damned." Carson shook his head. The crazy horse seemed to prefer the domestic life. A thoughtful look crept into his eyes. Tess had spoiled the beast with all that TLC she'd poured on it. "She spoiled both of us," he admitted.

The sound of his voice echoed in his ears. He was going nuts, talking to horses, to empty rooms. He couldn't stand the silence.

He thought of the party yesterday. Tess. Honey-girl. All golden in her pretty dress with her brown-gold hair flowing around her shoulders. The smooth, silky feel of her in his arms.

Pain gripped him all of a sudden, squeezing his heart so it was hard to breathe. It hurt to think about her. Last night she'd been so cool, flirting with him but laughing about it, as if the situation between them didn't matter at all.

A game. She'd been playing a game last night...to conceal the hurt he'd inflicted? An image rose in his mind. Tess, dressed in jeans and sweater, working in the house, cleaning out the stables, tending that stupid, spoiled stallion as if he were royalty.

Had she been playing then? Had she? He searched for the answer, trying to ignore the clamoring of his heart.

No.

The truth came to him with shattering clarity. When she'd come to him, she had been sincere, a woman in love, wanting to help her man.

During the crisis with the dam, he'd watched her

and the other two women going about their work—whether it was cooking, driving a truck or helping load bags with rocks—and had marveled at it. They'd worked as hard as the men. And after the men were finished, the women worked on, serving up food and cleaning the kitchen.

And then he'd seen Tess at the party—the beautiful, spoiled heiress. Except she wasn't spoiled. She was beautiful, she was stubborn, she was opinionated, but she wasn't spoiled.

She'd offered him everything—her love, her devotion, her hard work, her knowledge of ranch life. And he'd thrown it away.

God, he'd been so wrong. His pride hadn't let him see her as a woman willing to carry her share of a marriage.

He closed his eyes against the sting of tears. Grown men don't cry. Unless they've ruined their lives. She'd never take him now. He'd hurt her too much and for too long. How much forgiveness could a man expect from a woman?

A whicker drew his eyes back to the outdoors. The stallion rubbed his nose on the flank of one of the mares, then he mounted her.

The call of the blood or hormones or instinct, whatever. It was real. The stallion would stay, Carson realized. The animal was willing to give up freedom for companionship, food, care and security. Looking into his own dismal future, it didn't seem such a bad exchange.

He'd give anything to have Tess back in his home. The realization was like the dawn creeping up on a dark world. He'd thought the ranch was everything to him. It wasn't. It was just a pile of rocks and dirt. Tess was…Tess was life itself. To lose her was to lose the very essence of living.

Why had it taken him so long to see it?

He banged his fist down on the counter, angry with his own stupidity. Then his eyes slowly swept the kitchen. It looked nice with the new curtains and fresh paint, with the soft patina of gleaming oak.

Tess's doings.

He'd faithfully watered all the plants she'd left, chiding himself for his ridiculous feelings about them. He realized that intuitively he'd felt if the plants lived, then maybe…

He grimaced painfully. Yeah, he loved her. Always had. Always would. Once, she'd loved him. Dammit, she would again! He'd go after her, bring her home where she belonged.

After the way he'd treated her? Why the hell would she want to return? His shoulders slumped momentarily, then he had an idea.

Striding to the telephone, he dialed a number. "Ramon, do you know how to put in a sink and lay flooring?" he asked when the man answered.

"I have done the first and seen the other," Ramon said carefully, not sure what his boss was getting at.

"Let's get with it then. Come on over after breakfast."

When Ramon arrived, Carson had the old chipped sink out. Together, they got the new one in and hooked up. It only took them two tries to stop the leaks. The flooring took a bit more effort, but after reading the instructions—and arguing about what they meant—they finished the job by late afternoon.

After thanking Ramon for his help, Carson headed for the shower. It was Saturday. Did she have a date? His face hardened. He was going to go over there anyway. He'd wait if he had to. Forever.

Tess led Patches into the stable. After taking care of the horse's needs, she headed for the house, her book under her arm. She'd spent the day out by herself and felt somewhat renewed.

Like the giant who'd had to touch the earth to retain his strength, she mocked herself. She'd needed the solitude after the party last night. After seeing Carson.

She pressed her lips together and fought a battle with tears. She was not going to think about him. He was the past. The future awaited her.

With rapid steps, she went to the house and took a shower. After blow-drying her hair, she slipped into fresh jeans, a T-shirt and her old loafers from high school days. Lainie and Dev were getting ready to leave when she descended the short flight of steps to the front hall. Davie was watching a TV show.

"Sure you won't change your mind and come with us?" Lainie invited, a worried pucker between her eyebrows.

Tess shook her head. "You two go on. Have a good time. Tell the Moreleys hello for me."

"Put Davie to bed at eight o'clock. He was up late last night." Lainie pulled a shawl around her shoulders.

''If he gives you any trouble, sit on him,'' Dev advised.

''Aunt Tess wouldn't, Dad,'' Davie said, giving away the fact that he'd been listening to the grown-ups rather than his show. ''She's *nice*.''

The adults laughed.

''I guess that means I'm not,'' Dev admitted wryly. He dropped an arm around his wife's shoulders. ''Ready, love?''

''Yes. See you later. There's a lot of stuff in the refrigerator for your dinner,'' Lainie advised.

Tess put a hand on each of them and propelled them out the door. ''We can fend for ourselves. Out with you. Have a good time,'' she called, closing the door behind them.

She watched them leave, feeling their love for each other and for her and Davie long after they drove off to have dinner with a neighboring rancher. She joined Davie in the family room-office for the rest of the TV show. When it was over, she stood and stretched. She realized she was hungry.

''Okay, sport, let's raid the kitchen. Last one there is a rotten banana!''

She waited until he was ahead of her, then charged after him, both of them laughing when they dashed into the kitchen in a tie.

''I won,'' Davie declared, breathless.

''It was a tie.''

''Was not.''

''Was, too.''

She flipped on the light, dispelling the shadows of

the gathering dusk. A gasp escaped her when she saw a person standing on the other side of the screen door.

"Carson," she said.

He looked so serious, so...she didn't know what... grim, maybe. Hurt? Or angry. That was probably it. He was angry. With her? She angled her chin into a stubborn tilt.

"I was just going to knock when the stampede started. I didn't think you'd hear me over the noise. Davie won. He was ahead by an eyelash when you got to the kitchen."

The light tone didn't go with the intensity of his gaze. A premonition of trouble snaked through her.

"Oh, well, in that case, you can have the drumstick if there's only one left," she said, conceding the race to her nephew. She glanced at Carson, still standing on the patio. "Come in. We're about to eat supper."

"Leftovers," Davie added when Carson stepped inside, taking his hat off as he entered. "You want some?"

Bless his generous little hide, Tess thought, trying for amusement, trying not to let her heart tremble.

For a second she remembered other meals when Carson had sat across from her and they had talked, or argued, about his ranch and her being there. The too-ready tears surged into her eyes. She didn't want Carson near her, not anymore.

"He probably has other things to do," she said to Davie. She looked at Carson. "Anything we can help you with?"

He nodded. "There is a problem."

She wished he wouldn't watch her so closely. It

was making her nervous. His thoughts were unreadable as usual. It didn't matter anymore, she reminded herself. *He* didn't matter anymore. However, they were neighbors.

"What is it?" she asked. "Do you need Zed or one of the hands to help you?"

Carson shook his head. Looking into Tess's wary gaze, he realized this wasn't going to be easy. Gone was the tenderness, the soft adoration. He suppressed a groan. He had to get her to his place, to show her the Appaloosa, to tell her how much they needed her. The desperation of failure goaded him on.

"The stallion," he said, his tone rougher than he'd meant. "He needs you."

"The stallion?" she repeated. "The Appaloosa?"

"Yeah."

"He's back?" Before he could reply, she demanded, "Is he hurt?"

Carson hated to lie to her. Her compassion for her fellow creatures was so absolute, she felt their pain. Tess, gentle, kindhearted Tess. Once she'd loved him as much. He tried to hold on to that and not think of possible failure. His life depended on her abiding love.

"Yeah, he's hurt."

A worried frown settled on her forehead, nicking two little lines between her eyes. "What's wrong?"

"I'm not sure," he said slowly.

Tess saw a muscle move in his jaw. He probably hated having to come over and ask for help. The stallion must be pretty bad. "Has he gotten into barbed wire again?"

"No, there're no obvious wounds."

"Hmm, loco weed," she diagnosed. "Lupine. No telling what he got into." She clasped her hands together over her chest. "Do you think someone poisoned him? An angry rancher..." Her voice wobbled to a stop.

"That's possible. Will you look at him? You're the only one who can get close." Carson clenched his jaw at this lie. Would she hate him for the subterfuge? Remembering the hostile glance she'd given him when he'd arrived, he didn't think she would come with him willingly. And he was determined she would come with him.

"I'm staying with Davie." She was careful not to say *baby-sitting*. That always provoked an argument with her young nephew, who loudly protested being called a baby.

Carson looked at the boy and smiled, a solemn smile of unexpected sweetness.

Tess felt it clear down to her toes. No, no, no, she wasn't going to feel that way about Carson.

"You should have called first. It would have saved you a trip over," Tess told him.

"Rose can stay with me," Davie volunteered. "She's fun."

"Thank you very much," Tess muttered.

"You are, too, Aunt Tess," he added, anxious not to hurt.

Tess fixed a plate for Davie and stuck it in the microwave. "I really can't go. You know as much about treating animals as I do." He really did, she said to herself, trying to appease her conscience. But what if the horse dies? it asked. "I'm too tired," she added.

"You went off on Patches with a book," Davie reminded her, his lower lip pooched out a bit. She hadn't taken him with her.

"Eat your dinner," Tess said. "We'll discuss it later."

Davie sat down at the table. Tess looked at Carson. He obviously wasn't going to budge. He stood there like a gangly cowboy, hat politely in hand, and waited for her. The grim expression on his face told her he didn't want to be there anymore than she wanted him to be. The situation must be serious.

"Call Rose," Carson said.

"She's probably busy."

"Call her," he snapped, his patience at an end.

Tess rounded on him. "Don't come in and start giving out orders. You're not the boss."

"Okay. I'm sorry. It's just that...I'm a little on edge." He ran a hand through his hair. "I'm worried." His smile was forced.

Against her will, her heart softened. He did look worried. And tired. And angry. Dear God, would she never get over him? She closed her eyes, heard him move. When she opened them, he was standing next to her.

She felt his heat the entire length of her body. A shiver ran over her. Her body remembered other times when they'd been close. She whirled away. "I'll call," she heard herself say.

Just because of the Appaloosa, she told herself. She couldn't let the animal suffer simply because of her own cowardice. She was afraid of being alone with Carson, she admitted.

She stalked to the phone, dialed and heard Rose answer. ''Hi, this is Tess. Sorry to intrude, but... something's come up. Would it be possible for you to come over and stay with Davie?''

''Is that Carson's truck in your drive?'' Rose demanded.

''Yes.''

''I'd be glad to stay with Davie.''

''Listen, if it's too much trouble—''

''It's not.''

Tess sighed. The fates were against her. ''Thanks, Rosie. I'll do the same for you someday.''

Rose laughed. ''I'll be there in two shakes.''

Rose arrived in three minutes. ''Don't worry about a thing. I'll tell Lainie where you are.'' She cast a furtive glance at Carson's glacial features and Tess's set face. ''What's going on?''

''The Appaloosa has been poisoned,'' Tess explained. She pulled on her work boots and gloves. Grabbing a light jacket she headed for the door. ''I'll be home as soon as I can.''

''Take your time,'' Rose called after them.

''You didn't kiss me good-night,'' Davie shouted. He ran onto the patio. Tess kissed him and exchanged bear hugs. She waited while Davie kissed Carson, too. Carson had a strange look on his face when he straightened to his full height. She couldn't read the emotion in his eyes when he glanced at her, but it made her feel peculiar. As if she were close to discovering some great truth if she would but think a little harder.

Outside, Tess cast an eye on Carson's old truck. "I'll drive one of ours. That way, you won't have to bring me home."

Carson took her arm and propelled her to his vehicle. "I'll get you home," he said between clenched teeth.

He opened the door and thrust her into the seat with big hands around her waist. "Well, since you put it that way," she muttered.

Carson got in. He reached out and briefly caressed her shoulder. "Thank you for coming."

His voice was so unexpectedly tender, she felt like crying. Darn it, she was supposed to be over him. She turned her head and stared out at the twilight. It still wasn't completely dark when they reached his ranch.

"Where is the stallion?" she asked wearily as soon as he turned off the engine.

He got out and came around to her side. Opening the door, he motioned her out. "This way."

She clambered down on her own, ignoring his hand.

"Don't be afraid of me, Tess."

"I'm not." She looked him in the eye to show him. His gaze slashed into hers, all the way to her soul. There was a waiting quality about him, she saw. It confused her. "Well?"

"Over here."

He led her around the truck and toward the stable. She saw the Appaloosa at once. His distinctive coloring showed up against the dark brown of the two mares.

"Where did you find him?"

"He came back on his own...willingly."

"Oh." The way he said *willingly* seemed significant.

They walked over and leaned on the railing. "In fact, he insisted. He jumped in the corral and wouldn't leave."

"He did?" She couldn't believe it. She eyed the stallion. "He doesn't look sick."

The stallion danced around a bit, making a show of coming forward until he was close. He stood still, looking at them. When Tess didn't touch him, he batted her hand with his nose.

"He's missed you," Carson said.

"He's missed his oats and hay." She scratched his ears.

"And your grooming him and scratching his ears. The funny way you croon at him when you're working. He missed all those," Carson insisted. He paused. "That's what's wrong with him."

Tess swallowed hard and kept her attention on the horse. "He's not sick at all," she said with growing comprehension. "it was a—a trick to get me over here."

Anger instantly replaced the worry. Carson had let her fret over this dumb horse all the way over, and look at him...any fool could see the stallion was in his prime. And felt it!

"You lied," she accused.

Carson nodded, his gaze never leaving her face.

"Watch this," he said. He went to the truck and returned. He tossed an apple in the air. The stallion caught it. Juice flew all over Tess's face when he crunched down on it.

"Oh," she cried in irritation, wiping at her face.

Carson whipped out his handkerchief and dabbed the droplets. She went very still under his ministrations.

"Close your eyes," he said. She did. He gently wiped apple juice from her eyebrows and lashes. Then he kissed her, a brief touch of his lips to hers.

"Don't." What was he trying to do to her? She threw his hands off. "I want to go home."

"No."

Pivoting on one foot, she faced him, squared-off for combat. "Your little trick isn't funny, Carson. I don't know why you got me over here, but you can take me home—now."

The imperious Tess Garrick of the imperious Garricks. He felt an overbearing tenderness for her. He swallowed against the knot of fear in his throat. She had to forgive him, to see that she belonged here with him and the Appaloosa. Where were the words when he needed them?

"I want to show you something."

Tess stared at him suspiciously. He sounded almost humble. Was that apology in his eyes? Ha! Since when had she ever been able to read Carson McCumber's emotions?

Clamping her lips together, Tess let him guide her toward the kitchen door. They walked across the granite.

"Close your eyes," he said. "Please."

Damn, he felt like a kid, so anxious to impress her. Well, he *was* anxious to impress her, he admitted.

Sighing in exasperation, Tess closed her eyes. He led her forward. She heard him open the door and was aware of the brightness against her eyelids when he turned the kitchen light on.

"Come in," he said, and led her forward. When they stood in the middle of the floor, he told her to open her eyes.

She did. The room looked vastly different. She glanced at him, puzzled. This was the important thing he wanted to show her? This was why he had lied to coax her over to his place?

"You got the vinyl installed." She admired it from several locations in the room. "It's beautiful, Carson, really lovely." She waited for his next move. Her pulse began to speed up a bit.

"Ramon and I did it," he said. "We only came to blows twice trying to figure out how." His wonderful smile flashed over his mouth. He waved a hand around the room. "It's all your doing."

"Not all of it," she murmured, disconcerted at the look in his eyes. She was afraid to believe what she thought she was seeing. His emotions had so rarely been visible for her to read. Except when he was angry with her. "Oh, you put a new sink in, too."

"Umm-hmm. Think we're ready for a spread in *Better Homes and Gardens*?" He seemed so... anxious. A tiny ember blazed to life inside her. What was he really saying?

"At the very least. This is wonderful." She gave him a tentative smile and saw his fist unclench.

"Next, I thought a dishwasher right under here, close to the sink." He indicated the place.

"That would be convenient."

"Would it?"

"Yes." He was suddenly very close to her. She backed up a bit. He followed. All pretense left him. His smile disappeared. She saw his eyes roam over her and recognized the flames of passion in his eyes. A letdown kind of emotion ran through her. So that was what the strange evening was all about.

She turned her back and walked toward the door. "I'd like to go home." Her voice came out strained. She knew her control was slipping due to the powerful longing he generated in her. When would she stop reacting to him? When she was ninety, maybe.

"Don't go," he said, his voice dropping a register.

She stopped, her heart beating painfully against her ribs. Oh, heavens, she was going to cry. No she wasn't. Biting her lip, she fought the tides that raced through her. She wasn't going to let him do this to her. She whirled.

"What do you miss, Carson? My cooking and cleaning? The chores? Or the way I was always willing to fall into your arms at the least encouragement?" Tears filmed her eyes. She blinked them away angrily. "I'm not that girl anymore."

"No," he agreed. The words came hard for him. "You're a woman now. The woman I want."

"Tough. I'm not available." She slammed out the door, her heart pounding in rage and hurt.

He caught her before she stepped off the granite. "Tess—"

"Let me go." She fought with him, trying to break his hold. He refused to budge. He held her wrists in a loose but unbreakable grip. Finally, when she gave up, he swooped and lifted her in his arms. Startled, she threw her arms around his neck.

"That's better." He frowned and carried her back into the house.

The old Carson had returned, the one she knew so well, who always got his way, who was always telling her to get out and stay out of his life. Except now he was forcing her in it.

"I don't understand you at all," she snapped, glaring right back at him.

He went into the living room and dumped her on the sofa. Then he lit the wood already stacked into a pyramid in the fireplace. When he was sure it had caught, he turned back to her. He curled his fingers into fists, then forced them open upon his knees. He rubbed his hands against his thighs while he thought.

He looked at her with grim determination. "It's simple. I love you."

"Ha!" She crossed her arms over her chest, holding herself together by sheer willpower.

"It's true."

"When did you discover this great fact?" She was *not* going to fall into his arms just because he mumbled a few words...and grudgingly, at that.

"Recently. It's been there all along, just as you knew it was, but I was too...stubborn to admit it. I was afraid, Tess."

That almost got to her. Her defenses wobbled before she remembered the facts. "You? I don't believe that for a second." Carson McCumber had never been afraid of anything, not even her brother that time when she'd been sure Dev would kill Carson.

He gave an exasperated sigh. "Dammit, it scared the hell out of me. To love you was to take a chance on losing you. I couldn't do that."

"Why would you have lost me, for heaven's sake? I loved you, too." His reasoning made no sense to her.

Silence lengthened between them. "I had nothing to offer you. I thought you'd get tired of the life here," he said at last.

"Never," she vowed, angry that he could doubt her love. She'd been steadfast in it for so long, how could he doubt her? Tears sprang into her eyes. She dashed them away.

Before she knew what was happening, she was lifted into a pair of masculine arms again. Carson set her across his lap. "Don't cry, honey-girl. I can't stand it," he growled in a low, fierce tone.

"Let me go, Carson," she demanded, struggling.

"Answer one question first. Do you love me?"

"Yes. Now let me go."

"Never," he said.

"I answered your question. Let me go."

He looked incredulous. "Why should I let you go now? You love me. I love you."

He seemed to think that solved everything. She pried at his fingers, trying to loosen their hold on her.

"What's wrong with you?" he roared, finally out of patience.

"You! You're what's wrong with me," she shouted right back. "You love me now. You believe in my love...now. But what about tomorrow? What if someone runs off with your blasted cows and you don't get them back? What if a tornado sweeps down and wipes out this place? What then?"

"What are you ranting about?" He gave her a little shake.

Tess felt the movement of his thigh muscles under her. It stirred impulses in her she'd like to have ignored. Heat spread in rippling waves throughout her body.

"If you lose everything, do you send me back home again?"

"No."

"Do we use my money to start again?"

He didn't answer.

"You want to give everything, but you can't accept anything from me. What kind of partnership is that?"

"I wasn't thinking of a partnership. I'm talking about marriage," he told her.

She touched the spot over the bridge of his nose where the frown lines cut the deepest. "What am I allowed to contribute?"

"Tess," he began, trying to find a way out of this morass. "I don't want the Garrick money. I want you, only you."

She thought it over. The money wasn't important to her in itself. She didn't need it to live happily with Carson, but she saw he had a need to make it on his own. She could save it for their kids and grandchildren. Still, they needed some accord on the subject.

"If I wanted to use some for a trip to Europe, would that be okay?" she asked.

He obviously thought the question strange. "Yes," he said.

"Would you go with me?"

Another pause. "Yes."

"Can I use it to start my line of pedigreed cow ponies?"

He frowned thoughtfully. "I suppose."

"Would you mind if I had the outside of the house painted? And maybe insulated the attic?"

He glared at her when she grinned. He grinned, too. "Do whatever you want with the damned stuff," he murmured on a low groan. "How soon can we get married?"

"A month."

"No way."

"A week."

"Let's go to Vegas."

"How impetuous you are."

His hands began to roam over her. "I've waited five years."

Tess closed her eyes, the lonely years rushing through her like a cold wind. The fire crackled in the hearth, warming the chill of evening that had crept over the house with the setting of the sun. Carson's arms warmed her.

She stopped his roving hands. "Sunday after church."

"Tomorrow? Great." He sighed in relief.

"I meant next week. We can't get a license tonight."

"Yes, we can." He inhaled the sweet, clean scent of her.

"The courthouse is closed."

"I'll bribe the clerk. If that fails, there're always threats."

She laughed. Reaching up, she touched his face with trembling fingers. Was she dreaming?

Carson recognized the wariness in her, saw the hesitation in her eyes. Once she'd given her trust to him freely; now he'd have to earn it. He'd show her, he vowed, with a lifetime of love.

Chapter Eleven

The congregation was astounded when the pastor invited them to stay and hear the vows of Carson McCumber and Tess Garrick after the regular service was finished.

"Well, I never," Mrs. Vickers said loudly enough to be heard in the last pew. She was visiting with her son and daughter-in-law, who lived on a nearby ranch.

Everyone stayed.

Carson entered from the pastor's study. He nodded to the organist, who launched into the wedding march. Dev, Lainie, Davie and Tess proceeded down the nave. Dev took up a position beside Carson as best man. Lainie was matron of honor. Davie had declared himself best boy and no one had the heart to tell him he couldn't stand up with them, too.

After the brief ceremony, Carson lifted her

mother's wedding veil from Tess's face and kissed her. She was beautiful in a flowing white gown. An angel. His to love forever.

Dev invited the whole church to dinner at the ranch. Half the town had been invited the night before after Carson had roused the court clerk out of bed and talked him into opening the office. It was a joyous occasion. Mrs. Vickers got tipsy on champagne and smugly told everyone she had known the wedding was bound to happen. She'd seen the writing on the wall long ago.

The afternoon sun was on the wane before the wedded couple pulled up in front of their home. It was decorated with wild flowers and yards of crepe paper.

"The Montagnas," Carson said. He lifted Tess out of the truck and carried her across the granite slab into the house. He didn't set her on her feet until they were in the living room.

The fire was already laid in the grate. He set a match to it. Then he turned to Tess. He kissed her, gently. His passion was great, but he was determined to go slowly with her.

"Would you like to change?" he murmured against her hair. "Rachel left us supper in the oven. Are you hungry?"

Tess moved her head from side to side. "Let's not wait any longer," she whispered. "I've loved you for so long, so terribly long."

His heart swelled. She sounded almost sad. He pulled her to his chest, cradling her against him, needing to give her comfort. "I know, honey-girl. I know."

He felt sad himself. Perhaps it had to come to this point before he could appreciate all that she was—good, loving, sincere, hardworking.

She turned her head. He saw she wanted his kiss. She opened her eyes. It was all there. For him. Adoration. Love. All the devotion a man could want.

"Tess," he said, desperate for her to believe him, "I love you. Let me give you my love."

"Yes. Oh, yes."

Tess gave him back kiss for kiss, each one sweeter than the one before. She became dizzy from so much sweetness. For a long time, they kissed. He explored her mouth, his tongue eager for the taste of her. She did the same to him.

Then kisses weren't enough.

His fingers paused at the pearl buttons on her dress. She held her breath. Slowly, he began unfastening them. He pulled the material off her shoulders. She stood very still. His eyes went very dark when her breasts were revealed to his questing gaze.

The silk floated to the floor. The rest of her clothing followed. She sighed raggedly and watched as he peeled his clothes off and tossed them aside. He turned to her.

He cupped each of her breasts in his hands, so gentle and careful with her. He squeezed, then rubbed until her nipples stood out against his palms. He bent and kissed one, taking the tip into his mouth and sucking.

Spirals of strange sensation shot through her. She

clutched his shoulders, then stroked his skin, liking the warm, smooth feel of it in her hands. Restless, she ran her fingers through his hair. He changed to her other breast and licked and sucked it into a hard bud. Finally, he laid her on the sofa where they had come so near this particular bliss before.

He caressed her from her waist up, over and over, until she was ready for the next step.

She looked at him, at his beloved face where a fire burned in his eyes and his lips waited to take hers again, at his chest where dark hair grew in a sexy pattern leading downward. She let her gaze follow, saw the stirring her perusal aroused in his body.

She studied him there where he seemed the most powerfully masculine and wondered at the marvelous structure of the body.

"I won't hurt you," he promised.

"I'm not afraid. I've never been afraid of loving you," she said, realizing it was true. Her only fear had been that he would never love her back.

Her gaze swept the long length of his sinewy legs. They, too, were liberally covered with the dark hair she found so exciting. She lifted her hand and touched his chest.

"Tess," he said, a groan of need.

"Touch me, Carson. Touch me now," she pleaded.

He caught her to him. The world became concentrated in the space they created between them. She knew nothing but the wonder of his touch, the thrill of his lovemaking. He was very patient and very thorough.

"Love," he whispered when she cried his name,

needing him more than she could have ever imagined. "Can you take more?"

"Yes." She ran her hands over him, stroking along his back and hips, free to express her love at last.

Careful with her, Carson eased deeper into the warm cocoon of their love. Looking into her eyes, he wondered why he had ever doubted her love, why he had thought an easy life was the only one she could take. She was like the land itself, always there, waiting for him.

She moved under him, raising her hips to meet his thrusts, bringing him ecstasy he'd never known. Time slowed. He was aware of only her. He tried to give her as much pleasure as she gave him. When she went still, then cried his name, he could hold back no longer. Together they found their bliss.

"I love you," he said a long time later. They lay cupped together on their sides, looking into the fire.

"I love you." She stroked his hand, which rested intimately just below her breast. She sighed.

"What are you thinking?" he asked. His voice was lazy, replete with their lovemaking.

"Do you really want to know?"

He raised up on one arm and peered into her face. "Yes."

"Here she lies, where she longed to be..." She broke off with a soft laugh. "Where she'd longed to be for years."

"Was it what you...expected?"

"It was everything and more."

She heard him sigh contentedly as he lay back

down. He had given her the sun and the moon, but he still worried that it wasn't enough. She'd show him it was. She had a lifetime to do it in.

* * * * *